To: Diam

with

from:

Stephen (Reggie) Solomons

CHARLIE'S WAR

Stephen Solomons

Pen Press

First published in Great Britain by Pen Press

All paper used in the printing of this book has been made from
wood grown in managed, sustainable forests.

ISBN13: 978-1-78003-101-9

Printed and bound in the UK
Pen Press is an imprint of
Indepenpress Publishing Limited
25 Eastern Place
Brighton
BN2 1GJ

A catalogue record of this book is available from
the British Library

Cover design by Jacqueline Abromeit

Dedicated to Christine, Melissa and Julianna.

About the author

Stephen Solomons was born in Ceylon and spent his formative years on his father's tea plantation. He has lived in England for nearly fifty years. He worked as an administrator at the University of London and the Lord Chancellor's Department as a caseworker at the Court of Protection. Now retired, he lives in Selsdon, Surrey.

course. Whatever it is, I can assure you it will be a vital exercise in our efforts to defeating the enemy.

'From now on our training will be on survival techniques. Our training will be in gruelling conditions. You will be trained to be experts in the use of explosives and demolition techniques. How to use camouflage and to be able to live off the land. By the time you finish your training, I expect you to be tough, rough and a mean bunch of men capable of dealing with all contingencies. Our aim is to be a specialist fighting unit that will strike terror in the hearts of the enemy. We have an important job of work to do. I will be counting on you men to do a thoroughly fine job and acquit yourselves in an honourable way.

'Right, let's have your names starting with Robert Crawford.'

'I am Bob to all and sundry and I come from Darwin in Northern Australia but to those of low intellect I am generally known as Crawfie.' There were sniggers and snorts from the men.

'Crawfie will do but to assume we are of low intellect is patronising. We can do without that. I will settle for Crawfie.'

'Elvis Samson from Trinidad.'

Elvis stood up and took a bow. 'I am called Elvis by my family, sir.'

'Good. Elvis, you may sit down.'

'Brandon Curtis from Barbados.'

'Brandon you may also sit down.'

'Ade Adewoke from Nigeria.'

'Ade will do for us. Thank you.'

'Kristen Maake from South Africa. I prefer to be called Maake.'

'Next, Scott Campbell from New Zealand.'

'I am called Scottie by my friends.'

'Thank you, Scottie.'

'Charlie Digby-Sloan is the name and I'm from Ceylon. Charlie is fine by me.'

The roll call continued. Freddie Jones from Canada, two English men, both cockneys from the East End of London, John Smith and George Gray, an Irishman Eddie Murphy and a Scot named Dougal Macfarlane who preferred to be addressed as Dougie.

'I was expecting a baker's dozen but I guess I will have to settle with what I have been given.

'Right, now that we all know who's who, I will continue. Let us start as we mean to go on. First we dispense with formality. We will use your chosen first names. It is good for team work and the boosting of morale or so I'm reliably informed, but for all of you, you may address me as Sir.'

There was a titter of laughter.

'We leave for Dartmoor as soon as transport can be arranged. We will live under canvas and simulate some, if not all, the conditions you are likely to endure. I can assure you the food will be better than that served in our mess. Dry rations and canned bully beef will be the order of the day.'

There were a few groans to be heard.

'On the plus side there will be no square bashing.'

A murmur of approval greeted this announcement.

'Make no mistake, we a have a tough job ahead of us. That is all for now. Any questions?'

Before any were asked, the captain said, 'Good. That is all for now. You make take the rest of the day off.'

The captain left the room as smartly as he had entered it.

'Struth, mate, that was short and sweet. You heard the man say we had the day off. I'm off to town, anyone care to join me?'

'I'll tag along, Crawfie,' said Charlie.

'If there is a pub count me in. I hate this freezin' cold and a warm fire is what I want. That and a warm dame.' Brandon was smiling in anticipation.

'You'll be lucky,' chipped in Scottie.

'Warm dame? More like warm beer is the most you will get around here,' snorted George.

'George is right,' agreed John.

4

'I'll settle for a warm dame and no beer,' laughed Elvis. 'I don't know nothing about warm beer and warm dames but I'll tag along with you guys. Any place is better than this camp.'

'Where do you think this special assignment will be?' asked Eddie.

'By hearing what is on the news, most likely France.'

'I doubt it, there are no jungles in France or Germany, and only deserts in North Africa, so it is more likely to be South Asia and the Japs. I hope it is South Asia. Those yellow bastards are raping English women and children and killing their men folk.' Dougal was visibly incensed. 'I signed up to get a crack at them.'

'I did the same, Dougie. I want a crack at them too,' said Charlie.'

'What's the point in guessing? We will soon be in the thick of something particularly nasty,' said Crawfie. 'Let's get something to drown our sorrows. English ale, Scottish whisky, French brandy, Russian vodka, Irish Guinness, whatever is available, I will drink it. Booze is booze. I'm not fussed. I'll drink the lot. Let's get the hell out of here.'

While they waited for transport to Dartmoor, the men made the White Horse their regular 'watering hole' each evening in the cosy saloon bar with its open fire.

Crawfie was the talkative one who regaled them of his exploits around Darwin. He said he craved some action so that was why he enlisted. What he actually meant was there were not many unmarried 'sheilas' to his liking. He prided himself as a ladies man. English roses, he had heard, were missing their sweethearts who had gone off to war. Crawfie was brash and cheeky, and the girls he 'chatted up' found him amusing, but boredom on civvy street was another matter. So he did the next best thing and joined the army.

Some weeks later the team gathered for a briefing from their leader. They had been moulded into the tough, rough and mean bunch of commandos in the desperate conditions they had faced on the bleak moors of Dartmoor.

'Men, our moment for glory has finally arrived. Our destiny has been defined for us. The moment has come to stamp our mark in history. To do our duty for King and country. Whatever happens, may your God bless you, and if that fails put you faith in your rifle, your bayonet, your explosives, or any improvised weapon you can make because the name of the game is survival at all costs. I promise you this will be no picnic in the park. Watch out for your comrades and I am sure they will watch out for you. We work as a cohesive unit or we will fail. We have trained hard but that alone will not be enough. You will need to call on your sixth sense, animal cunning, and your strong sense of survival in a harsh and dangerous environment if you are to survive. I am hopeful the comprehensive training we've undergone over the past few weeks will be of benefit when put into practice over next few weeks.

'Our politicians bleat on that it costs a fortune for this privilege. Our number one priority is to give the enemy hell. Fail and we perish. Our mission has started. There is no turning back. Let's give these bastards a taste of their own medicine.

'Many of you may have guessed by now as to where we are going. We are off to Burma you lucky lot. We will be fighting in the jungle. Our principal enemy are the Japanese. But there is also disease, flies, leaches, snakes and elephants, tigers and leopards to name but a few.

Captain Robert Lee paused as looked around the room. 'It's not all doom and gloom. We are going to have fun and maybe good times too, and build up a repertoire to tell our grandchildren as we bounce them silly on our knees.' Another pause, his smile was replaced with seriousness. They had arrived in India by troop ship and transferred to Delhi two weeks ago.

'We leave tonight at 20:00 hours and reach our drop zone an hour before dawn. The weather reports are favourable. Remember the drill and hopefully all will go to plan. A few pointers to bear in mind. After the drop, we regroup as quickly as possible. Make sure your parachutes are gathered and well hidden. Obliterate all signs that might give our position away. We've practised the drill long enough. Do your work quickly and efficiently. Remember the Japs are well trained, cunning, and deadly in an environment that is strange to us and they will be waiting for us. Do not underestimate the enemy. Let's hope there won't be a reception committee waiting for us. Deal with any casualties first, then dig in and wait till first light, then we will get our bearings and proceed from there. Is that clear?'

The captain looked around the room. His men were attentive but he also detected some nervousness in the ranks. Some fidgeting and scratching of chins and heads.

'We will be behind enemy lines. Our orders are to gather intelligence of enemy activity, and to get this info back to HQ via our radio link. I have also been advised that drops of rations and ammo will be made, but to be quite frank, I don't think we can rely on this happening. We shall do our work as professionally as we can, and remember, we are not expected to win this war single-handedly, but to try and lessen the odds whenever and wherever possible, but it is vital to get whatever info we find back to the allies. We will engage the enemy where and whenever we can but only when the odds are in our favour. This may not always be the case. We will deal with each situation as we see fit.

'Obviously, we are heavily outnumbered so we will have to be unconventional at times to avoid being killed. Hit and run tactics would be our best options and this is where your special training and skills will be put into operation. Our best bet is to pick our moments where the vegetation is dense, and visibility is poor to get close enough to dispatch the enemy with maximum surprise, then disappear just as quickly from the scene to regroup for the next skirmish. If guns are to be used we will use them but only in a kill or be killed situation. It is vital to keep this operation covert.'

Captain Lee paused again.

'Make no mistake our task is a difficult one but I know I can count on you to do your best. One of our objectives is to harass the enemy wherever possible to stop their advance. Sabotage. We will disrupt communication lines, blow up bridges, roads and railways, ammunition depots and fuel dumps, and while doing this we will be gathering the vital intelligence to help those following in our footsteps. Any info we are able to give our allies, the better the chances of bringing this war to an end and saving many lives. Of course it is a tall order and some of us may not survive, but that is precisely what we are here to do. I have tried to give you as clear a picture as I can of the mission ahead of us. Any questions?'

'Do we take prisoners, sir, and if we do so, what do we do with them?' came an enquiry from the back.

'With an operation such as this, I'm afraid that situation will not arise. I don't think I need say more. From the information to hand, the enemy has flouted all the rules of the Geneva Convention and we will take them on by their own rules. I must reiterate that we have not one enemy but two. The Japs and the jungle. Never underestimate either. The jungle is as deadly as the enemy. They are both killers.

'I have spelled out the dangers that await us. Be alert and vigilant at all times. Your life and that of your comrades will depend on you keeping your wits about you.'

'What about supplies, sir?'

'As I said before, I wouldn't rely on that too much. If the planes can get through we have several drop zones and times when drops will be made. It is up to us to rendezvous at these spots when the drops are made. Intelligence tells us there is much activity in the area so those bastards could be waiting for us. We know the Japs have got their eyes on taking India and Ceylon, and like Singapore, it will most probably be overland. It's the logical route if they are to bring in personnel and supplies. Our main concern is to get as much intelligence as we can and pass it on to the allies. The US and British Navies have blocked the sea routes but if we can slow them down till our main forces get to them, well and good.'

'What contingencies are in place if supplies are not forthcoming, sir?'

'There are no contingencies. But if our mission is to succeed, it will only do so if we have adequate supplies. We must try and ensure we get these supplies. Apart from that little detail everything should be hunky dory.'

Not being able to get supplies had crossed Captain Lee's mind but he did not wish to dwell on the fact that without guns, ammo, explosives, food and medicine for his men, his mission would be a lost cause.

'Dougie, make sure you have additional packs of quinine in case of a hitch. If we run low on rations we survive off the land. I'm reliably informed the peasant farmers hate the Jap invaders but are afraid to collaborate with Allied Forces for fear of reprisals. We could get lucky. We could also try the Buddhist monks if all else fails.'

'Sir, the country is tropical like Ceylon so the rivers will be teeming with fish and the jungle plentiful of fruit, vegetables and meat,' stated Charlie confidentially. 'We won't die of starvation. Bullets and diseases yes, but not starvation.'

'You wanna bet, mate. The Guv said this ain't gonna be a picnic. Without ammo we're dead, unless, of course, we take the weapons off the yellow bastards we kill. Either that or make bows and arrows.'

'Naw, we take the kit off every bastard we kill. What we can't carry we cache it. Go back for it when we need it.'

'It's called thinking on your feet.'

'It's called survival, man. Ain't you learned nothin' man. Like Dartmoor.'

'Shucks, I forgot to pack my fishing tackle,' came another wise crack from the back to the amusement of all gathered.

'Starving to death never crossed my mind but tropical fevers are something else.'

'We can hijack Jap supply trucks, matie.'

'But will you eat dead and rotting dog meat?'

'Meat is meat, man, if it is cooked well. But rotten meat, no way man.'

'Dog meat and a side salad will do fine for me if I was starving.'

Captain Lee waited with an amused smile on his face listening to his men. He had come to recognise it was their way of relieving tension in this way. He waited until the banter stopped.

'Charlie. Would you like to add anything that might be helpful to the task ahead? For those of you gentlemen who are not aware, Charlie is our expert in jungle lore having cut his teeth in the jungles of Ceylon.'

'I wouldn't call myself an expert but I can mention a few titbits to titillate the thought processes of my friends gathered here today.'

There were a few boos and whistles.

'Okay, padre, keep the sermon short and don't waste good drinking time.'

'Bless me, Father, and I promise not to sin again.'

'Come on chaps, settle down, let's hear what Charlie has to say.' Captain Lee brought the room to attention.

'South East Asia has a lot of dangerous animals in their jungles. Tigers, leopards, bears and elephants, plus all kinds of poisonous snakes to name those that could do the worst to spoil our party. If you encounter a tiger or leopard, you shoot it with a bullet to the head. Kill or be killed. They are far more dangerous than any Jap you will meet. These animals are silent killers and blend in with their surroundings. They are known to stalk their chosen prey for hours or even days if they are hungry. The tiger will kill you, not necessarily to eat you but to hone its skills, and because you have entered its hunting ground and are threatening its food supply. The leopard is nocturnal and secretive, and therefore not much is known. But dangerous too. The bear is not as clever and as cunning as the two mentioned and can be chased away with a lot of shouting and arm waving unless it has made a kill and is guarding its meat. It could be quite ferocious and it would take on the tiger and the leopard and sometimes fight to the death.

'Elephants are herbivores and they have no need to kill to eat but will guard their young fearlessly. Move away from the herd quietly and move slowly. Make no eye contact. Eye contact denotes aggression. If there are elephants in our area it is best to rub some fresh dung on your legs, arms and faces. All animals have an acute sense of smell. They will accept you as one of them. Tigers, leopards and bears very seldom attack elephants.'

'Charlie, how do you deal with snakes?'

'With extreme caution and a lot of respect. Snakes are killers too. A cobra bite will kill you in minutes. However, they will only bite humans if we tread on them or suddenly startle one. I can cope with cobras but there are two types of viper that we call the *polongga* in Ceylon. They lie in wait and kill for the sheer joy of killing. They will kill you in minutes too.'

'Charming. I must remember to write that down in my diary.'

'Oh, and I must also mention the scorpions while on the subject of nasties. Eight to ten inch long centipedes, and leeches during the wet season. Rubbing soap on your legs and up to your upper thighs helps until the soap gets washed way.'

'What's best in jungle food or bush meat as it is called in South Africa?'

'Plenty. Wild suckling pig roasted on a spit. Duck, wild fowl, cranes, crows, cormorants, monkeys, iguanas, squirrels, rabbits etc. Tastes as delicious as the food served at the Savoy or in Chinatown, especially if accompanied with yams, and garnished wild herbs and vegetables. At a push you can even sink your teeth into a snake.'

'So what can we expect for dessert?'

'You guys are never satisfied I see. Well, there is mango, bananas but we call them plantains in Ceylon, and these come in a wide variety of shapes and sizes, paw paws, guavas, berries. The list is endless, unless, of course, the monkeys, fruit bats, squirrels and birds don't get them first.'

'Bloody hell. If not for the Japs, the tigers, the leopards, the bears, the elephants, the scorpions, the poisonous snakes, the flies, the mosquitoes and those blood-sucking leeches, our lives could be an exotic experience,' Crawfie waved his hand in disgust. 'Struth, mate, if this is to be our contribution to this bloody war, it is going to be mighty exciting.'

'You said it, matie.'

'You heard it just the way it is.' Charlie had had enough. 'My lesson has ended for today, brethren. And I have kept it short with no frills and no fuss. Warts and all. As the Guv said, practise starts bright and early tomorrow.'

'Frills? Warts? You've got some lady friend. You must introduce to me to her.'

'Thank you, Charlie, for your enlightening and informative lecture. Are there any more questions of a serious nature?'

There were none.

'For those of you who wish to commit sin, get drunk, visit bars and brothels, do so now. Those of you who wish to pray, I'm sure there is a church nearby. Good evening gentlemen.'

CHAPTER TWO

The expatriates in Ceylon went about their daily lives like they had done before Chamberlain declared 'a state of war with Germany' existed on 3rd September 1939 following the invasion of Poland by Hitler's troops.

The war in Europe was something they kept at the back of their minds because it did not affect them in any way. A few luxury goods were in short supply but there was plenty to eat and drink. The ballrooms and bars were crammed, and they were able to go to bed without a care in the world.

But all that was soon to change with the dawn raid on the American Pacific Fleet in Pearl Harbor on Sunday 7th December 1941 by Japanese fighter planes and bombers. Now the Americans were at war too. The Japanese, like the Germans were hell bent on over-running island after island in South Asia. The British Protectorate of Hong Kong was captured ten days later, and Singapore fell without much resistance on 15th February 1942.

Suddenly it became clear that matters had become extremely serious for the people of Ceylon and drastic steps had to be taken to stop the Japanese from invading their little island. Like Singapore, Ceylon too commanded a strategic position in the Indian Ocean and to achieve their objective, it was argued, the Japanese needed to capture Ceylon if they were to get their hands on the riches of British India. The newspapers reported that the Japanese planned a two-prong attack imminently. One from Ceylon by sea and the second pincer from Burma, overland, to secure their objective. It was obvious to everyone, but the scaremongering from the screaming headlines made many people extremely nervous.

The Japanese presence was too close for comfort. The British and her allies too were making preparations to halt the Japanese advance. They had to retake Singapore at all costs.

Charlie, like many of the islanders and the expatriates, had decided to enlist. He was going to fight for the country he loved and a way of life that was now under threat. He was young and free and it was his responsibility to defend his birthright from all comers and do whatever he could, however small, to protect his parents, brother and sister from a fate that befell those who had been conquered.

If anyone from his family had to put their life on the line, it had to be him. His brother, Rupert, and Jenny, his wife, could take over Glencoe, the tea estate he managed, to help his father and increase tea production to help the war effort. His sister, Kylie, was still at school. Also, the moment had arrived when he had to break free from an emotional entrapment that was doomed to end in disaster if it continued in its present form. Another reason. He would fight for King and country. He decided he would sail to England and enlist there.

The woman standing almost six feet tall in opened-toed shoes caused much interest as she walked into the hotel. Philip Webster was no different to the other men in the hotel lobby as his mesmerised eyes followed her sinuous and sexy saunter to the reception desk. He was instantly smitten. The woman had an almost perfect complexion that came from the sun and salt air of a long voyage under blue skies. There was an aura of radiant health and animal magnetism one associates with that of a slinky cat.

Penny Lesley had shiny red hair that tumbled onto her shoulders and seductively clung to her throat, framing a face with high cheekbones. Luminous green eyes hinted to a sensitive yet vivacious personality. The sometimes quizzically raised eyebrow, or the widening of her lips in a smile, or the toss of her hair, suggested a secret something that many a red-blooded man found intriguing, sometimes exciting, and most emphatically tantalising. She had the air of a woman who knew what she wanted and went after it when the mood took her fancy. She was a woman who knew how to project herself to the object of her desire. There was no doubting she could be a threat to most women.

Penny became aware of the effect she wielded on the opposite sex long before she grew up into womanhood. Philip Webster was no different to the other men who had come into contact with her. Seeing her walk into that hotel lobby with her long, suntanned legs, made him put his newspaper down. The flowery summer dress she wore reminded him of those worn by the ladies who visited the Royal Botanical Gardens at Kew on warm summer days where he started his career in horticulture soon after university.

In her hand was a wide-brimmed straw hat similar to those he had seen being hawked around Mediterranean ports, which she had taken off on entering the building. He observed her unhurried walk to the reception desk, looking neither left or right, she spoke briefly with the receptionist, picked up her room key, smiled as if he was the most desirable man on the planet, and was gone in a flash.

Perhaps the heat was getting to Philip Webster. He had just seen the most attractive, adorable woman he had ever seen in his entire life, and now she was gone like a fantasy of his imagination. He sat there for a long time hoping that if he did not move the vision he had seen would not fade from his mind.

Philip had finished his business meeting that had brought him down to Colombo an hour earlier, and took a rickshaw to his hotel. He had also noticed the *Adrianna* come into the

15

Port and stopped idly to watch the passengers come ashore in motor launches and get out at the jetty. Philip assumed Penny was one of those disembarking to see the sights, and instead of returning to the ship, was a guest at his hotel. On enquiring he was told the *Adrianna* was due to leave for Singapore and Australia the following afternoon.

Philip was a confirmed bachelor but today he felt strangely elated. No, a tinge of excitement had crept into his eyes as he planned on the possibility of trying to get acquainted with his vision of beauty. If he was successful, it would be the highlight of his trip to the capital. No, it would be the highlight of his very existence. He seldom left the hill country, preferring the cooler climes to the heat and humidity of Colombo. Was this some special omen that conspired him to be at the same hotel as this woman, his apparition from heaven?

Neither Philip nor Penny knew that a meeting would present itself later that evening. Perhaps the Gods were being kind to him.

Most of the guests who were staying overnight at the hotel had had their dinner and gone up to their rooms or were still exploring the nightlife the city had to offer. Penny, like him, had wandered into the ballroom to listen to the latest music from Europe being played by the six-piece band, and to watch the few couples who had taken to the dance floor. Philip had contrived to find seat close to where Penny was seated.

Presently she became aware of the tall, bespectacled Englishman who kept looking at her shyly and turning away when she returned his look. There was something about him that intrigued her. She guessed that he was either an archaeologist or perhaps an explorer. He was too tanned and weather-beaten to be a colonial administrator who spent long hours in an office. It was obvious he was single. She could tell at a glance.

On the spur of the moment, she decided she would make his acquaintance. The evening was boring and she had nothing to lose by doing so as she would be off to Australia the next day. It did not bother her if he thought she was being too forward or pushy. Penny had nothing to lose by being friendly to this shy Englishman and it could be interesting. Another anecdote of her travels to relate to her Aunt Agatha. A fellow countryman seemingly stuck on this small exotic island many thousands of miles away from England.

She got up from her chair and made her way to the ladies cloakroom passing close to him. As she came abreast, she looked at him and smiled, and was not surprised when he smiled back. She had broken the ice. Penny decided she would engage in conversation with him on her return.

'Hello, I couldn't help but notice you sitting there with no one to talk to. Are you waiting to board the *Adrianna* tomorrow? I hadn't noticed you on board before,' Penny smiled.

Philip rose to his feet. 'I'm afraid the answer is no. We seem to be the only two singles whiling away an evening. Would you care to join me?'

'Thank you, I would love to. I would like to find out what a fellow countryman is doing on this beautiful island. I tend to be a curious creature, and have been warned that curiosity could lead to trouble. See what it did to the cat.'

Penny smiled, tossed her hair and sat down next to Philip. Her smile instantly relaxed Philip. His shyness gone. His boring evening promised to become a very interesting one.

'Travelling by oneself can be boring at times.'

'Not for me. My trip so far has been really interesting. I'm travelling on the *Adrianna*.'

'To Singapore or Australia?'

'Australia. Primarily to visit my aunt. I'm intrigued to know what brought you to this island.'

'Oh, the usual thing, work. Have you had an opportunity to explore?'

'This is my first and only venture outside the British Isles, and unfortunately, my ship leaves tomorrow so any exploration is out.'

'Perhaps, I can be your guide on your return journey.'

'My intention is to settle down in Australia so that counts me out. A pity. I've heard so much about its beauty, friendly natives, and of course its exotic food. One of my travelling companions on the *Adrianna* came over to marry a tea planter. She seemed to know so much considering she had not set foot here before.' Penny laughed. 'Fancy that, she is very courageous or very much in love. Anyway, thanks very much for your kind offer.'

'Well, you've missed a wonderful experience.' There was genuine disappointment on the man's face. She also saw the loneliness in his eyes.

'I know. My loss. We cannot have everything we desire. We have to compromise and be thankful for what we have, and thank the Good Lord for all His mercies is what the nuns drilled into me since I was a little child.'

'Oh, by the way, my name is Philip Webster.'

'I am pleased to make your acquaintance Mr Philip Webster. My name is Penelope Lesley. My friends call me Penny. Not very original,' Penny laughed apologetically, her eyes twinkling mischievously.

'My friends call me Philip. It is always Philip, not Phil. I loathe being called Phil.'

'That's fine by me, Philip. I consider you as my friend. Don't you find social formalities, though necessary at most times, can also be so dreary at other times, especially when time is so short? You know how it is. You get to meet someone who interests you but you have to follow these social graces, and before you get to really know them they are gone.'

'How refreshingly frank. Penelope is such a pretty name but I will address you as Penny from now on, as I too am your friend. May I get you a drink?'

'Oh, I would love a drink. A cold glass of fruit cordial would be most welcome.'

Philip beckoned to a white-uniformed steward and ordered two glasses of chilled passion fruit.

'Have you tasted passion fruit before?'

'No, but it sounds promising.' Penny's expression made Philip laugh.

'If you think this drink is going to live up to its name I'm afraid you are going to be disappointed. Sadly, it has none of the qualities of an aphrodisiac.'

Penny joined in the laughter, raising one eyebrow in her inimitable way that made her look flirtatious. 'Now I am disappointed.'

'But the drink is exceedingly refreshing, don't you agree?'

'Excellent. Tell me, Philip, my curiosity has got the better of me again. What do you do here?'

'I grow tea for my livelihood. I don't reside in Colombo but up in the mountains.'

'Oh, that explains the healthy tan. Growing tea sounds easy but I suspect there is an awful lot more to it before we see the end product in our cups.'

'The process is fairly straight forward. Our cuppa, as the Cockneys affectionately refer to it, has to go through a series of processes before it is ready for the teapot, but I won't bore you rigid with the details. If you are going to settle down in Australia what are hoping to do? Marry a rich Australian gold miner, a rich industrialist, or a sheep farmer on a huge ranch with no near neighbours for hundreds of miles?'

'Marriage is the last thing on my mind. My primary intention is to live close to Aunt Agatha who is quite frail. She is a widow and lives in Sydney. My Uncle Graham died a few years back but she refuses to come and live with me in England. So the next best thing is for me to go there. When the offer of a teaching appointment came up, I jumped at the opportunity.'

'A teacher, eh? The teachers in my school were never as attractive as you.'

'If that is a compliment, Philip, thank you.'

'It was a compliment. You must have the patience of Job.'

'Why?'

'You need lots of patience to be a good teacher.'

'I did not claim to be a good teacher. The governors of St Matthew's School for Girls assumed I was one.'

'I am sure you have all the right qualities and qualifications to be an excellent teacher or else they would not have given you the post.'

'More flattery,' Penny opened her eyes wide provocatively and smiled. 'I like it. Flattery, it has been said, will get you everything so please don't stop, Philip. St Matthew's School for Girls, I was told, is ultra-exclusive and very expensive. If my salary is anything to go by I guess I was very lucky in getting this position. Aunt Agatha has so much to say about Australia that none of her letters has stopped her singing its praises. She has convinced me there is a good life to be had out there. Just like she and Uncle Graham had. Anyway, I was not making much progress where I was, and nor were other matters going the way I thought they should, so I felt a change of scenery was needed. This job was just the impetus I needed to make the break. So here I am on my way to jolly good old Australia. My journey so far has lived up to all expectations.'

'You make it sound so permanent, Penny.'

'Nothing is permanent in this life, I can assure you, Philip. If things do not work out I can always return to England.'

'If things don't pan out the way you want it, and you pass this way again will you permit me the pleasure of your company again? I could show you around this island. Perhaps I could show you around my tea plantation up in the mountains.'

'Thank you, Philip. I will certainly take you up on your kind offer if things don't work out quite the way I have planned and I come back this way.'

Penny Lesley was aware how well the evening had progressed. Philip Webster was a revelation to her. Relaxed and easy going. He had come alive and the loneliness she had first seen in his eyes was no longer there. She liked his easy manner and found his conversation stimulating.

The conversation flowed easily and as the evening passed and Philip began to realise that he had fallen in love with this attractive young woman who the fates may have conspired to wrench away from him. The band had packed up and the ballroom long deserted before they retired to their respective rooms in the early hours of the morning. They had arranged to meet for lunch the next day.

Lunch was enjoyable too, getting to know each other more. But when the time came for Penny to make ready to return to her ship, there was no mistaking the sadness in Philip's eyes.

After exchanging addresses and promising to write to each other, Philip watched her get into her rickshaw and head towards the Port.

A few hours later he saw the ship heading towards the horizon and disappear out of sight.

CHAPTER THREE

On a cold, damp and foggy February morning in 1902 Brett Carter arrived into this world. Born into an ordinary middle class family, he was the youngest of three siblings. Mrs Carter had had a difficult pregnancy, and when she went into labour it was extremely painful and prolonged. The baby she gave birth to was very weak and blue in the face. It was touch or go whether the baby would survive. The medical staff spent some time to resuscitate the almost lifeless body, but as soon as it showed a spark of life they placed him in his mother's arms.

Major Harold Carter was to see his son and heir a week after the baby's arrival. He was a man to whom the army meant everything and took priority over his family. He was brusque, bombastic and serious by nature, and to describe him as humourless would have been an understatement. He strutted into the hospital briskly, his swagger stick under his left arm as if he was about to inspect his soldiers on the parade ground.

'Hello, Mavis, old girl. I have been informed that we have a boy at last.' There was a hint of pride in his voice. 'Well done. Jolly good show. A chip off the old block, eh? What? We've been waiting a long time for this moment. Good of you to oblige, my dear. I shall name him Brett, or perhaps, Bradley. No, let's stick with Brett. Brett Carter has a punchy military ring to it, don't you think, my dear? General Brett Carter of the Royal Hussars. Having the right name in this business always helps. Nigel or Adrian or Percy does not sound military somehow. To me those names are rather sissy, wouldn't you say?'

It was a statement rather than a question. Major Harold Carter lifted the shawl off the sleeping baby in the crib by his wife's bedside with his swagger stick as if to make certain his latest offspring was male.

'Yes, Harold, if you say so, dear,' replied Mavis Carter smiling tiredly at her husband, knowing that there was no room for argument or dissent. 'Don't I get a kiss for the effort I made? Brett is a nice name for him if that is what you want. He's not a strong baby and had much difficulty in breathing and barely made it. Had to be resuscitated, you know. The medical staff are to be congratulated for their skill in saving the poor mite. They told me he could fade away at any moment.'

'I'm not in the least bit surprised. Look at that bloody miserable weather outside. It's bad enough to give my old bones the shivers. Give the little beggar a chance. He looks perfectly all right to me. Midwives like to make a big song and dance to show how important they are and what good jobs they are doing. Of course you deserve a kiss but not right now. There's a time and place for that sort of thing. I shouldn't worry too much. He is bound to get strong as he grows up. He has only just been born. I'll see to it. Don't worry your little head about that now. I have reason to believe that our little boy will be perfectly fine in the months to come and grow up to be a fine upstanding young man in the years to follow. You mark my words. Unlike some of the recruits we get these days. Bloody wimps and layabouts. But we sort them out pretty damn quick. We get their arses out on the parade ground and soon lick them into shape. My regimental sarge tells them to shut the fuck up, and get the fuck out or he will kick the shit out of them.'

'Remember where you are, Harold. You are not on the parade ground now so please watch your language.'

'Pardon? What was that you said?' Major Carter tweaked his moustache and made a grunt while adjusting his swagger stick under his arm.

'Nothing, dear,' replied Mavis. 'It does not matter.' She looked at her husband and smiled meekly.

'We tried damn hard for that boy. Nearly damned killed me. I had to put a lot of effort into that exercise.'

'Tell me about it. I was there. Your face had gone the colour of purple and you grunted and gasped like pig after a bucket of swill. And you nearly had a heart attack too.'

'You think you had a hard time but we got the result we wanted at last.' Harold Carter gave a loud snort. 'It's the bloody horrible stodge that's being served in our mess. Have you noticed I've put on a lot of weight recently?'

'That fact has not escaped me.'

'But we cannot put the kitchen detail on a charge. More's the pity. But there will be none of that hanky-panky from now on. The name Carter will pass down the line and into the annuls of history for generations to come.'

'If that is the way you want it there will be no quibble from me,' Mavis said relieved that she would not have to go through that short-lived and horrible experience again.

'Must get his name down for a good public school right away. There are some specifically geared for direct entry to Sandhurst, you know. The sooner the better. There is no time to waste. Being in the right school always pays the best dividends. Preparation and character building is of paramount importance. The rest will follow naturally.'

'Yes, dear, whatever you say. You are always right.' The sarcasm in Mavis's voice was ignored by her husband. She felt sorry for her new born son.

'General Brett Carter. Yes, Brett has the right ring for such a high rank. The more I think of it the better it sounds. One has to aim high and instil the right standards from day one, so to speak. Picking a good name is important if my son is to make a name for himself.'

Major Carter bent down and pecked his wife on the cheek. 'Well done, old girl, you played your part to the best of my satisfaction.'

'I'm your wife. I had no choice.'

'Nonsense. Oh, by the way how are the girls doing?'

'Mrs Hoskins from next door is looking after them. She is good with them. I don't know how we would have coped otherwise.'

'Fine, fine, excellent. Remind me to pop in and thank her.' Major Carter appeared distracted and failed to grasp the gravity of his wife's concern for her other children. 'Jolly good show. What? Must go. Must get back to the regiment. Bit of a flap on. Kitchener has got us all jumping through hoops. Likes to keep us on our toes. Says it's good for morale. He wants his men to be mean and keen but he has failed miserably with most of his officers on that score. Most are either drunk or whoring or both.'

'All right, Harold, but do try to see to your daughters till I get back.'

'Will do, Mavis, but unfortunately duty calls so I must dash back to the regiment. Be seeing you soon, dear. Look after yourself. Bye, bye for now.' Major Carter saluted his wife, turned round and left the room briskly as if he was still on the parade ground.

'Bye, bye, Harold. Aren't you going to kiss your son goodbye?'

Major Carter did not hear his wife. He was already out of the door.

Major Harold Carter was attached to the Household Cavalry. His father died in action while holding the rank of Brigadier in the Seventh Hussars. He was waiting for his promotion to Colonel which he thought was long overdue. He expected his son Brett to follow in their illustrious footsteps and keep the family traditions. There was going to be no choice for his son.

Like his grandfather and father, Brett's life had been mapped out for him on the day he was born. The public school his father had chosen for his son and heir was well known for its sporting activities. Rugby, hockey, swimming, polo, rowing, cricket and athletics were part of the austere regime each day. The participation in outdoor activities took precedence over everything else. Education and the arts came a poor second.

For Brett, unfortunately, he preferred poetry and painting to the harsher body contact sports that the school took pride in pursuing. From an early age it was evident that he had inherited the qualities of his gentle mother. She did not subscribe to the brusque army way of life but tolerated her husband's idiosyncrasies while ignoring his father's insensitive nature and heavy handed manners. She saw that her son was gentle and sensitive like her from an early age, and she tried to shield him from his father's unreasonable expectations. She empathised with his artistic inclinations, and even encouraged Brett in his endeavours. This may have led to the confusion and anxiety that was to affect him in later years.

School days for Brett were unbearable, and it was a period of his life which he hated but had to endure. The requirements of the sports field were tough and demanding but somehow he managed to get by. What he hated most was bath time. He was compelled, like all the other boys, to take daily cold showers whatever the weather. His house master described it as being part of the character-building process. A strengthening of the body and the disciplining of the mind. An essential process of building one's moral fibre if one was to be a leader of men.

Despite Brett's complaints about what he thought was his harsh treatment, his father insisted it was the right school for his son, with an excellent track record for direct entry into the military academy at Sandhurst. They would knock the stuffing out of his effeminate nature and prepare him for a career in the army. It was his father's wish and there was no other way forward.

Brett did not see much of his father even when he was at home during his school holidays. On the few occasions when he did see his father, he was treated like one of his raw recruits. His father demanded that his son was neat and tidy at all times. Hair cut short and brushed back, his clothes clean and his shoes polished. If his father had any love for his son, he never made a public demonstration of it. Whatever affection Brett got came from his mother to whom he turned to fill the void left by his absent and unloving father. His two sisters were much older than him and they too excluded him from their activities. So Brett chose to follow a solitary existence at home or seek the company of his mother from an early age. She was the only person he could count on, and depend on, for moral support and comfort.

One day, Brett was summoned to the headmaster's study; a day he was never to forget. 15th April 1912. He had been tinkering with his crystal set when there was a break in transmission for a news flash saying the steamer, *Titanic*, belonging to the White Star Line, had hit an iceberg in the North Atlantic Ocean and had sunk rapidly. The brief bulletin went on to say that due to the prevailing icy conditions of the sea, and the speed with which the stricken ship had sunk, it was highly improbable there would be many survivors. Unbelievable. Perhaps the announcement Brett heard on his temperamental crystal set was incorrect or garbled. Perhaps it was some other ship or the announcer had got the name of the ship wrong. The *Titanic* was 'unsinkable'. It was a fact. Everybody knew.

There was so much publicity before the *Titanic* sailed to America almost everybody had heard of this great ship that had cost millions of pounds to build and kit out, and was the flagship of the fleet. On the other hand, if such a calamity were to be true, many rich, influential and powerful people had suddenly gone to a watery grave. It was difficult to comprehend such a dramatic event ever happening. Whole families would have perished without trace. Surviving relatives left at home, utterly distraught. A bombshell that came without any warning. One moment they were alive and enjoying themselves in the most luxurious liner ever built, the next moment they were dead. Disappeared without trace in the icy waters hundreds of miles from home.

All this was going through his mind when the headmaster's summons came. He had no inkling as to why the head wanted to see him. As far as he knew he had no relatives sailing on that ship. The day had been dull and boring but he had avoided getting into any trouble.

Brett hesitated for a minute or so outside the head's door, then knocked three times and waited.

Nothing happened. He was about to knock again, more loudly when Mr Smithers opened his door and beckoned the boy in.

'Come, boy. Sit over there in that chair,' said Mr Smithers pointing to a chair next to his massive leather-topped desk, which was always cluttered with papers and books. 'You may be wondering as to why I wanted to see you?'

'No, sir.' Brett sat down in the chair as instructed and looked at his shoes.

'I will come straight to the point, Brett Carter. It's best that way. I am afraid I have very bad news for you. Brace yourself, boy. It's best this way.' Mr Smithers' voice was unusually soft.

Still Brett could not fathom out the reason to warrant a summons to the head's study. His previous visits always meant a beating on his backside for some infringement of the rules or getting into mischief. It could not have anything to do with the sinking of the *Titanic*, but the use of crystal sets was banned in his school.

Without thinking, Brett blurted out, 'I know why you wanted to see me, sir. Perhaps, it has something to do with the sinking of the *Titanic* in the North Atlantic Ocean with all its passengers and crew drowning in the icy waters.'

The head looked at Brett strangely. He had not heard the news of the *Titanic* sinking. What on earth was this boy babbling about.

'Where did you get this information? No, never mind. I have summoned you here concerning another matter.' Smithers hesitated looking at the boy seated in front of him was somewhat surreal.

He cleared his throat and continued. 'Brett, I regret to have to tell you your father died this morning. It was sudden and the medics think it may have been a heart attack. Your mother is on her way to collect you for the, er, funeral. I am sorry to be the bearer of sad news. Please accept my sincere and deepest condolences.'

'Thank you, sir,' stammered Brett unable to comprehend the gravity of what he had just heard. It could not be right. A dreadful mistake. His father was relatively young and so strong. No, to be precise, his father was as tough as old boots. He must have the wrong person. Brett looked at his headmaster again. He was deadly serious, but then his headmaster never joked. Then he realised his headmaster was talking to him.

'Brett, I do not think you understood what I just told you.'

'I heard you, sir, but my father cannot be dead. It must be some horrible mistake.'

'I can assure you there is no mistake. I can understand this comes as a terrible shock to you. I fully understand this news has knocked you sideways. If there is any way in which I can be of any assistance to your mother, to you and your sisters, please do not be afraid to tell me. Understand? Until your mother arrives, I suggest you go to your dormitory and wait there. You will be told when she is here. Also, could you please inform Robert Lee to report to me immediately.'

Brett nodded his head to signify he understood his headmaster's instructions and left the study, closing the door softly behind him.

First the *Titanic*. Now his father. One was unsinkable. The other indestructible. Unbelievable.

Major Harold Carter was buried with full military honours. The funeral took place on a blustery, icy cold afternoon with the rain dripping steadily from his mother's umbrella under which he took refuge. His mother did not weep. His sisters did not weep. Brett did not weep. There was a deathly sombreness that was all pervading. Even the firing of the guns as the coffin was being lowered into the ground sounded muffled. His family appeared to be strangers witnessing a stranger's funeral.

The day after his father's funeral, Brett went back to his school as if nothing special had happened. His mother and his sisters did the same. Their lives were to back normal as it had always been before this incomprehensible episode.

CHAPTER FOUR

All her children were special to Clara Digby-Sloan, but Charlie was her first born and a new experience for her. The golden haired baby with dark blue eyes gazed at her before it suckled at her breast, its tiny fingers clenching and unclenching as it drew its strength from her with every sip of milk he got from her. Watching him close his eyes and snuggle into her arms as he dozed off to sleep. Looking with wonderment at the miracle of life she had helped to create. She could see that Charlie would grow up to look like his father and she hoped he would emulate all the fine qualities his father had endowed in him.

Soon the baby grew into a young boy whose boundless energy got him into one scrape or another. Always eager for adventure. Always curious about the things around him. He had principles to defend, and underdogs to protect. In time he would stand up and fight for the things he believed in. Courage that would help him survive the Japanese in Burma, and with it bring honour and glory to his country, his family and to himself. But no one could foresee at his birth, in those dark blue eyes that a part of his personality would cost him his life prematurely.

Charlie could bash out a rousing tune on the piano but music was not his forte unlike his brother and sister. He was robust and extrovert and full of anticipation for the next adventure. He was ready for action when the chance presented itself.

'Charlie, you were told never to go into the jungle on your own. If Mummy finds out that you have disobeyed her she would very cross with you,' said Kylie, his youngest sibling.

'I knew what I was doing,' replied Charlie defiantly.

'Of course Charlie knew what he was doing,' echoed his younger brother, Rupert. 'Charlie is not afraid of anything, are you, Charlie?'

'Not even wild elephants, or leopards, or wild boars, or bears, or wild buffaloes, or cobras?' asked Kylie, daring her big brother to confess that he was scared of something.

'I told you, Kylie, Charlie is not scared of anything.'

'There are no wild elephants or wild buffaloes this far up the mountain. They live mostly in the dry zone where the land is flatter, or with just a few hills. Dad described their habitat as thorny scrub land. That's why their skins are so thick. Thorns don't hurt them. Wild buffaloes need marshy ground to wallow in to keep cool and you don't get that up in the mountains,' explained Charlie.

'What about the leopards, and the wild boars, and the bears, and the cobras? They are very dangerous and could kill you,' persisted Kylie.

'If you study these animals you will know that leopards are shy creatures. They won't attack humans unless they are absolutely starving, or defending their young or fighting for their own preservation. You can hear the bears and the wild boars if you are quiet. Simply move away from the area as quickly and as quietly as you can.'

'And what about the cobras? If they bite you, you will die.' Kylie was not going to be fobbed off so easily.

Charlie laughed mischievously. 'If you come across a cobra you stand very still and stare at it. It will stare back at you but after a little while it will get bored and slither back into the undergrowth. Cobras will only attack you if you frighten them, or accidentally tread on one.'

'I hate snakes,' Kylie's body shuddered in disgust.

'Kerry Stirling has snake eyes. He is such a bully. I must stare at him and hope he slithers away like a snake. He is much bigger than me and I am frightened of him. On second thoughts, I will avoid him like the plague.' said Rupert thoughtfully.

'We all get frightened, Rupert. The trick is not to show you are frightened. Next time Kerry tries to bully you, show him that you're not frightened of him.'

'But I *am* frightened of him, Charlie. He is so much bigger than me.'

'Try it. If it does not work I will show you a different way to deal with him.'

'Can you show me too, Charlie,' asked Kylie eagerly.

'Aw, what's the point? Girls don't fight.'

'They do some times,' insisted Kylie. 'But I'm frightened of going into the jungle. Can I come with you when you go in next?'

'The jungle is no place for a little girl like you. Don't you ever go in there on your own. That goes for you too, Rupert.'

'You bet I won't,' replied Kylie.

'Me too,' said Rupert.

A few days after returning to their boarding school after the Easter break, Charlie noticed some swelling and dried blood on Rupert's face. He knew his brother would do his best not to get into any fights. He would walk away from any confrontation. If Kerry Stirling was bullying his little brother he would have to do something to stop it.

'Been in the wars again, I see.'

'Kerry is a beast. He's such a big bully. He always likes to pick on me. I tried to give him a wide berth but it doesn't always work. I tried the cobra trick on him but that too did not work. You know, staring at him like you would with a cobra to show you are not frightened. But he biffed me on the nose anyway. What you told me does not work Charlie. So you watch out too because cobras can kill you.'

'Perhaps you are right, Rupert. Perhaps we have to devise another way to stop him beating you up. I have an idea. Let's see if we can find Kerry.'

'He is bigger than you, Charlie. You will get a bloody nose too.'

'Let's give it a try. We'll soon find out. Come on.'

The two brothers went in search of Kerry Stirling, Rupert rather reluctantly. His nose was still sore from the whacking he got from Kerry and he did not want a second dose of the same medicine.

When they located Kerry, he was playing marbles in the corner of the school quadrangle with three other boys. Charlie sauntered up to them, his hands in his pockets as if he did not have a care in the world and kicked their marbles deliberately as he went by. It had the desired reaction.

'Oi, you!' bellowed Kerry. 'What the bloody hell do you think you are doing?'

'What? Are you talking to me?'

'Yes, you heard me, Charlie. What the hell are you playing at?'

'Nothing. What's the matter?'

'You kicked my marbles.'

'So I did. You should not put your marbles where I'm walking, you silly oaf. What are you going to do about it?'

'I am going to give you a bloody nose, you silly clot.'

'Oh yes? You are a bloody coward, Kerry. A big lump of lard is what you are. You are nothing but a bully and a coward who picks on little kids. I'm not afraid of you, thick head. Come on, try me and see.'

Charlie held his ground as Kerry closed in on him, then stopped. He saw that Kerry was a whole head taller than him and heavier built.

'Oh, go on. Get away from here. If you do that again I'll give you bloody good clouting.'

'I'm not scared of you, you oversized bully. Look into my eyes,' ordered Charlie.

The two boys stared at each other. Kerry Stirling hoped Charlie would back off. Instead Charlie struck like a cobra. He pulled his hand quickly back, swiftly landed a hefty blow on Kerry's nose and watched him fall to the ground like a poleaxed ox.

'Come on, get up. I have a lot more where that came from. Do you want a bit more of the same?'

Kerry lay on the ground wiping the blood that had started to trickle from his nose.

'See what I mean, Rupert. Works every time. Leave my brother alone or I will give you two black eyes as well the next time you go anywhere near him. Understand?'

Charlie and Rupert walked nonchalantly away.

'You told me I should stare at him like you do with a cobra, and he would back off.'

'It usually works with cobras, Rupert, but Kerry is not a cobra. You see, cobras have brains. They have instincts which tell them it is sometimes safer to slink away. If they don't, you do the next best thing if the first does not work. You whack him as hard and as swiftly as you can before he can throw a punch. It's called surprise. Worked this time.'

'Cor, Charlie, you were not afraid of Kerry.'

'You are wrong, brother. I was scared stiff but the secret is not to show it. Now Kerry will believe I'm not afraid of him even though he is bigger and stronger than me.'

'If a wild elephant charges you, it is no good staring at it and hoping it stops in its tracks.'

'Quite right. If a wild elephant charges you, you run as fast as you can.'

'Perhaps I should have run away when Kerry came after me.'

'Yes, Rupert.'

'But isn't that being a coward, Charlie?'

'No, it's called self-preservation. That's what wild animals do in the jungle. Little animals have to be cunning or the big animals will get them. But big animals like wild elephants will not attack a leopard, or a wild boar, or a bear because if it did, it too would suffer injuries or be killed. You see, Rupert, these animals have learned to live in harmony with each other, giving the other its own space. They have learned over the centuries that there is enough room for all of them to live together in the same jungle. But that is not strictly true either. Sometimes hunger makes them do strange things.'

'I suppose you are right. I never gave it much thought. Perhaps Kerry will leave us alone now.'

'I think he will,' laughed Charlie relieved that his ruse had worked. 'I'm pretty certain he will unless the message has not got through his thick skull.'

Some weeks later, the children were playing in the garden when suddenly from above their squeals and laughter the terrified screams from one of the houseboys cut through the air.

'*Aiya parmbu, aiya parmbu,*' (master snake, master snake) from the direction of the orangery. Charlie's father took off running as fast as he could in the directions of the screams.

'Please stay where you are and keep the children with you,' his father shouted to the other parents, who were at their house for a children's party and who had started to follow him. 'I will deal with this.'

Charlie ignored his father's instructions and followed him at a safe distance. He saw his father pick up a long stick as he approached the snake. He saw the raised hood of a cobra poised to strike at the petrified houseboy. His father had to act fast before the highly venomous snake bit the houseboy.

'Be absolutely still. Don't move a muscle. Do as I say and you will be fine,' commanded his father in Tamil, speaking softly and drawing the snake's attention away from the servant. As it was about to strike, Charlie watched his father use the stick swiftly, and with one deft stroke sent the snake flying through the air. He then watched it slither way uninjured into the jungle. Had the snake bitten the houseboy, its deadly venom would have killed him in minutes.

'Well done, Dad. You were very brave. You could have got killed.'

'Not me but Raju would have been a gonner. I knew what I was doing, Charlie.'

'Why did you not kill it?'

'There was no need to kill. The snake was as frightened as Raju. It was important not to panic either of them. The snake was searching for prey and Raju must have got too close to it. The snake was defending itself in the only way it knew. Raju spelled danger to its life. In the jungle every creature has to fight for survival. Kill or be killed. Eat or be eaten. The snake was probably after frogs or small mammals. They also raid bird nests for eggs or the chicks. That is how it is in the wild. Now if I was a mongoose I would have killed the cobra and had it for my dinner, but I'm not a hungry mongoose.'

'I never thought of it like that, Dad.'

'Good, I'm glad I was able to teach you something of the wild today, son. We don't have to kill for the sake of killing. Raju is okay, and the cobra is okay.'

'And we have saved the mongoose his dinner for later.'

'Yes, but did you know snakes kill a few hundred people on this island every year, and a few thousand in India? But the Hindus have the snake as one of their deities. They also have the elephant, Lord Ganesh, and monkeys and other animals as their Gods. Did you know Raju is a Hindu?'

'No. But one of his Gods almost killed him.'

'Yes, I don't know the answer to that conundrum, Charlie. In some parts of the world human sacrifice to their deities is still practised. I, personally, won't sit in judgement as to whether it is right or wrong. There are all sorts that live in this world.'

'But we must not kill for the joy of killing.'

'Absolutely. One must always respect the nature around us which has taken millions of years to evolve. If we destroy the wonderful things around us, there will be nothing left for those who come after we have gone. Cobras are very dangerous. Make no mistake of that but there are other animals, and not necessarily in the jungle that are even more dangerous. It takes time and patience to learn the ways of the jungle but once you do, you can survive in the jungle for as long as you like.'

'I understand, Dad. Can you teach me?'

'Perhaps, when you are a bit older, Charlie, but until then, learn about the wildlife in our garden. There is so much to see in it. If you are patient, and you observe what's around you, you will appreciate the wonders that abound here.'

After a pleasant but tiresome day's teaching, Penny Lesley returned to her apartment to see a letter on the floor when she opened the door. She was surprised but instinctively guessed it was from Philip Webster before she picked it up and saw the sender's address on the back. She took it into her bedroom and placed the letter on her dressing table. She decided she would read it after she had something to eat, finish her chores and settle down for the evening.

Much later she returned to her bedroom, retrieved the letter, and lay on her bed to read it, but before opening the letter she scrutinised the writing on the back for some minutes. She noted that Philip's handwriting was slightly slanted but bold and clearly legible. A good sign. She could tell the personality of a person by their handwriting. Studying the subject as a hobby was something she had been doing for a long time. She did not always get it right, but when she did, it gave her much satisfaction to know that her theories in general do work.

As she read Philip's letter she became strangely elated, her mind wandering back to their chance meeting in Colombo. In his letter, Philip went into some detail about his home and the work he did on his estate. The name of his estate, Kandalami, sounded so exotic to her. So different and certainly nothing like the names in Sydney or in London.

That letter was one of many to follow. She found them quite interesting and as the months passed, she realised how eagerly she awaited for the next one to arrive. Like a schoolgirl waiting for a letter from a pen friend to arrive from a country that was a small dot on the globe thousands of miles away. A country that was warm and colourful with hidden delights to be explored. But to Penny the vivid image in the foreground was always the face of a lonely man.

Also, she felt she knew this man better than any man she had had a relationship with in the past. Soon, a closer intimacy developed with each letter, and the realisation that she was emotionally drawn to this shy, bespectacled, suntanned Englishman who lived on a little island in the Indian Ocean, was getting stronger.

Any reservations, or nervousness, she might have had about her teaching job at St Matthew's School for Girls quickly vanished as soon as she walked through the impressive high wrought-iron gates, with its school crest boldly incorporated into its intricate design. Penny was also surprised to discover the high standards there were comparable to any of the public schools she had taught at in England. Entry was through stringent written examination, not merely the ability to pay the high fees.

She settled down easily to the daily routines, though demanding, and derived much pleasure from her work.

Aunt Agatha, however, was a different matter. Although well into her eighties she was sprightly for her age, fiercely independent, and totally self-reliant. Her Australian accent and the many Australian expressions and terminology took some getting used to, but there was no denying her free spirit, which was an Australian trait.

Aunt Agatha was pleased to see her only surviving relative but at their first meeting she had no hesitation in spelling out the ground rules to be followed. She treasured her own space and there was to be no mollycoddling from anyone while she had some breath in her body, thank you very much. She was absolutely convinced that when her time came to depart this world, her beloved Graham would be waiting to welcome her into the next world. Penny saw how much she missed her husband by the way she spoke about him. Graham coped with everything life had thrown at him, and she has done the same, and would continue to do so in the future. There was no doubt in her mind when she said she and Graham had had a wonderful life together.

'You soon forget about the hardships and difficulties of those early years because the good memories linger on and the bad ones fade away. Your Uncle Graham was a determined man. Could be very stubborn at the best of times. I got to know that on the very first day I met him. No matter what I said once he had decided on something, nothing would shift him.'

Aunt Agatha would have a nostalgic look in her eyes when recalling their life together.

'I had to follow. There was no question whether I agreed or not. That sounds awful but I always chased dreams and most times I guess I was unreasonable. It didn't matter too much as most of his decisions seemed to work out. After we married, he took sole responsibility for my well-being. He knew I would follow him to the ends of the earth, and even to hell and back, if necessary. He strove to do the best for both of us. He was no quitter or a shirker. In those early years, Australia was raw and soul destroying at times and you had to be strong and learn to take the rough with the smooth. Oh yes, my dear. If you didn't have the right spirit it could have broken you. It finished off many a good man and woman I can tell you. Many did not survive the harsh conditions. Other gave up the struggle and returned to the old country. Some made fortunes, others lived on scraps.'

Aunt Agatha paused and drew a deep breath, casting her mind back for examples, then waved her hand as if to say it did not matter now.

'Still, I think it was a far better life than the hardships of London. At least it was for Graham and me.'

Penny would listen to her aunt without interrupting when she was in one of her talkative moods. Her beloved Graham would always be somewhere in her anecdotes. At such times Penny could feel the inner strength her aunt drew from her past to belay her frailty. She felt at times that she was intruding onto hallowed ground, a place of sanctity in her aunt's memories.

During her frequent visits to her aunt's modest house on the outskirts of Sydney, she would usually find her slumped deep in her rocking chair immersed in her memories. She was pleased to see her niece but what she could not abide was her niece's efforts to make things easier for her.

Penny's cleaning and tidying, or washing bits and pieces was frowned on, and occasionally firmly rejected. She wanted no encroachment on her independence.

Aunt Agatha would shout: 'Leave well alone girl.' Or, 'All will get done in good time.' Or, 'How did you think I managed before your arrival?'

Being misunderstood as an interfering busybody was the last thing Penny wanted, so she learned to temper her over-zealous inclinations so as not to upset her aunt.

Over the winter school vacation, Penny arranged to spend a few days with Aunt Agatha, making do in the little box room next to the kitchen. There was a bed in the corner surrounded by all sorts of bits and pieces that had found their way in there over the years. Her aunt was always going on about tidying the room but somehow it always got put off, and there was always a reason why she never got round to doing it. The room was cramped but Penny managed to make a space for herself. She wished the bed was longer because her feet hung out at the end unless she curled up.

41

Still, it was only for a few days. She was hoping to find out more about her aunt and uncle's life in Australia, and more importantly, about her own parents and her early childhood.

As far as she could remember of her own childhood was being surrounded by nuns at an orphanage. She learned to make do in that little box room. It was a pleasant time. She and Aunt Agatha would invariably have a light supper. Penny would do the washing up and they would retire to the front room, get a fire going, and make themselves comfortable for the evening. Most times there would be very little conversation so Penny would catch up on her reading and her aunt would knit or sew until it was time for bed. But when her aunt was in the mood to chat they would discuss many topics of interest.

'It feels nice and cosy in here,' said Penny stretching her long legs and rubbing her hands appreciatively. Her aunt would have her favourite shawl around her shoulders, knitting. 'What are you knitting?'

'A shawl. I find knitting rather relaxing. Perhaps, I will knit one for you as a present.'

'Thank you. I would like that very much.'

'The chair you are sitting in was Graham's favourite chair. He'd come in from work, kick his boots off and sink into it and be as happy as a doleful hound. No matter how much I nagged him about his boots it was the same every day. I suppose we both got used to that bad habit in time.'

'Aunt Aggie, please tell me about our family. There is so much I need to know.'

Her aunt continued with her knitting. Penny thought she had not heard her and was about to repeat her request when Aunt Agatha stopped her knitting. She looked at her niece for a moment, then put her knitting down on the floor and folded her hands in her lap. She gazed into the fire with a faraway look, then looked at Penny and smiled.

'We have to go a long way back,' she took a deep breath. 'I don't know how much you know. Where does one begin?'

'Tell me about how you and Uncle Graham first met.'

'Oh dear, it was such a long time ago. Did you know your grandpa was parson?'

Penny shook her head. 'No.'

'Yes, he was. We lived in a big rambling old house in a very poor part of Hackney. I can still remember to this day how cold it was even in the summer, but the winters were the worst. I could never get warm in that house. Now you know why I light a fire even if it gets slightly cold here. Oh, how I hated the cold. Ugh. I was the only child till your father was born. Your grandma said it was a miracle from God, being blessed with the creation of life after so many years. Your father was born when I was about 15 or 16. Your grandma gave up the ghost when your father was about four. The cold and damp had got to her. I don't know if you knew your father's name was Toby. We were all devastated by your grandma's passing away. Especially your grandpa. He was like a lost soul wandering around that old house looking for reasons as to why she died so young. He said it was not the Good Lord's doing but the damp and draughty conditions they lived in that caused her death. Those very same conditions were to kill your grandpa a few months later.' Aunt Agatha paused, the memories were still painful.

'Your father was a lovely baby. Like a living doll. I did all I could to look after my father and Toby. After mother went to live with the angels in Heaven, father lost the will to live. Soon he became very thin and poorly. Hardly ate much. He was a bag of bones when they buried him.

My little brother, your father, was christened Tobias. Yes, Tobias, but we called him Toby.'

'No, I did not know that,' whispered Penny.

'Your grandpa developed a racking cough and caught a chill one freezing November day while visiting some of his parishioners. One of the old dears from around the corner popped in to help with the cleaning and the cooking. We tried to keep at least one room warm but it was a constant struggle. I could tell my father wouldn't last the winter. He looked so gaunt and awful. He battled on till Christmas and took to his bed on St Stephen's Day. I can see it all as if was yesterday. Mrs Swainson, the name has just come to me, came in as usual and she had brought a bowl of chicken broth she had made especially for father. She was a sweet grey-haired old lady. By then father was reduced to eating mash potatoes and finely chopped vegetables. When she went up to his room with the chicken broth, he had passed away in his sleep. He looked so peaceful. It was the last day of January, a new year that started with so much promise ended so tragically. Then it started to snow heavily. I remember crying all day. My tears would not stop. Toby stayed by my side bewildered by all that was happening. Mrs Swainson said it was a blessing in disguise the Good Lord took him away.' Aunt Agatha looked forlornly into the fire.

'When Father died our only source of income went with him to the grave.'

'So how did you and my father manage after that?' enquired Penny softly.

'Oh, Penny dear, if you only knew what a dreadful time it was for us. There was nothing I could do to stop it. After taking care of him the way I did it broke my heart to see him taken away from me. There was nothing left for me to do except go into service. But I was not one little bit sorry to leave that parsonage. At least it was warm where I went, but I did miss our Toby dreadfully.'

'Was it difficult to find work?'

'No, I was a parson's daughter. Even though I was on my uppers, being a parson's daughter was considered to be respectable and trustworthy and I could read and write. I got a job as a house maid in one of those lovely houses in Bloomsbury. Very posh it was. There were three floors and a basement. When a vacancy came up, they made me governess. You see, being a parson's daughter they trusted me. They were very rich people but they were also religious and very good to me. I had to look after four children. Being a governess I had my own room on the top floor next to the nursery. But it was hard work and I never got to bed till very late. Mind you, the children were well behaved. I had no trouble from any of them.' Aunt Agatha rocked herself for a moment in her rocking chair.

'Was it there that you met Uncle Graham?'

'Yes.' She laughed brightly at the recollection with some amusement. 'I met Graham while I was governess in that big house in Bloomsbury. He came to fix a door that had come off its hinges. I did not like him at first. He was such a cocky so and so. Fancied himself as God's gift to women, laughing and joking and flirting with the female servants. But I wasn't having any of his cheek. I learned from one of the maids that he had taken a fancy to me straight away. Anyway, he found out about my daily routines with the children. You see, I took the children into the private gardens in front of the house to play games or to read stories each day when the weather was fine. He had the cheek of the devil to climb over the railings at the far end of the square and wait for me by the swings. I paid no attention, pretending not to notice him there but he was persistent. I told you Graham was determined. Anyway, I don't know if it was his roguish smile, the twinkle in his eyes, or the brogue in his banter that won me over. I couldn't help myself, I soon fell head over heels in love with him. I was a lost cause after that.'

'This is fascinating. So what happened next?' Penny was eager to hear how they progressed.

'We did a lot of talking, and dreaming in that square. Graham came from a large family, and he came from a place called Waterford in Ireland. All his family worked in the crystal glass industry and the wages were good. But Graham wanted to be a carpenter. As usual he had to be different from the rest. His mother could not understand why he wanted to be a carpenter when there was a good job waiting for him in the crystal factory. His mother used to say, 'I cannot for the life of me understand why you want to be a carpenter. I will never know why until my dying day, you daft little bugger.' Graham always laughed his head off when he mimicked his mother. He always replied that he wanted to do something different to the rest of the family. Anyway, it turned out there wasn't much work for someone who wanted to learn carpentry in Waterford. Besides, he did not want to be an ordinary carpenter but a master craftsman. He was determined to prove to his mother that he could do it, if not in Waterford, then somewhere else. So he came to London and became an apprentice, learning the trade for five years. When his apprenticeship ended he did odd jobs while looking for an opening in one of the famous workshops that supplied the big shops with beautiful pieces of furniture, made from good quality wood, for the rich and famous.

'On my day off, Graham would take me out dancing. We went to this Irish pub in the Holloway Road in North London. The dancing there was very different to the dancing that I saw at the big house. It was an Irish jig he taught me in that smoke-filled pub. Graham liked to dance after a pint or two of his favourite stout.' Aunt Agatha giggled like a little girl. 'I hated the stuff. It was so bitter it was worse than medicine, I thought at the time.'

'So what made the two of you end up in Australia?'
Aunt Agatha was not to be rushed. She would recall her life history in her own good time. After thinking for a while she continued. 'Oh, he courted me for months but we also knew we could not get married, although he asked countless times. Graham did not earn enough to support us, and the little money he earned he spent on having a good time. I had a good job, I had a good place to stay, I was warm and well fed, and above all I was secure where I was. The thought of going back to a cold, damp, draughty room did not bear thinking about in spite of my love for Graham. To give up my job as a governess would have been an act of madness. Not me. Would you have done?'

Penny said nothing but shook her head.

'We carried on as usual. We had to make do with the few moments we spent with each other on my days off. Then something very unusual happened. Graham came to see me at the big house. He had never done that before because I told him never to do so. I could see straight away he was excited and chirpy. He said he had important news for me.' Aunt Agatha stopped, waving a hand in the air dramatically.

'Come on, Auntie, tell me, what was this important news?' Penny asked excitedly.

'Give me a chance, girl. Young people these days are always in a rush. I cannot be doing with rushing at my time of life. Be patient and I will tell you in my own good time.'

'I'm sorry, but this is so fascinating.'

'Well, I was astounded. Graham was offered a three-year contract to work on building houses, but the job was in Australia. There was a free passage for him and his wife and free accommodation provided by the company for the duration of the contract. He told me Australia was the new land of opportunities, and for those who worked hard there were rich pickings to be had. Skilled men were in short supply and he could make a fortune for the both of us. New houses were badly needed for the huge influx of immigrants flocking there in search of a better life than Britain had to offer. The upshot was, the company that made this offer wanted a quick answer. He said he desperately wanted to go, but he did not want to leave me behind. He said we could get married right away and leave for Australia within the week.'

'This must have hit you like a bolt out of the blue.'

'To put it mildly it took my breath away. Knocked me sideways. Whacked me for a six. It took me a little while before the gravity of his news sank in. I told him to hold on to his horses for a minute or two. I was going nowhere. Graham held my hand and asked if I still loved him, and if I did, I had to make this decision which would change our lives forever. We were going nowhere at the moment. Stuck in rut. This was the big break we were waiting for. I needed to be convinced. It was all too much for me to take in. Graham put the onus on me, I had to make the decision, and there was no time to waste or the job would be given to someone else. I told him to go away. He said my love for him wasn't as strong as I claimed it to be. He said he would go but would be back and to meet him by the tradesman's entrance that night.

'I must have been going around in a trance for the rest of the day because everyone was enquiring if I was all right, or whether I had caught an illness. They said I looked very pale and drawn.'

Aunt Agatha stooped and picked up her knitting from the floor but put it down again.

'I can tell you, girl, I did not know whether I was coming or going. My poor head was spinning.'

'I can imagine your dilemma.'

'I got to the tradesman's entrance as soon as I could that night. Graham was waiting for me. He had been drinking. Graham asked me what I would do when the children I was looking after grew up? I'd have to find another situation. That I had a false sense of security. Short-term comfort for long-term suffering. I would be turfed out, and if I was lucky, go from one big house to another till nobody wanted my services any more. All I would have to look forward to was the workhouse and no one would care if I lived or died. I went through a night of much agony but by the morning I had made up my mind. The rest you know.'

Aunt Agatha bent down and took up her knitting again.

'What happened to my father after you left for Australia?'

'Ah, young lady, spare a thought for your old aunt. It's late and I'm tired. I will tell you about your father tomorrow night.'

CHAPTER FIVE

'Your uncle referred to me as a Protestant and I would call him a holy Roman Catholic. This may mean nothing to you but there are sharp divisions in Ireland between these two religious sects. We were not religious. Far from it, I'm sorry to confess. If the subject came up we would argue like hell trying to score points against each other. Ah, does this surprise you? Oh yes, we had some fierce arguments, and the odd spat to clear the air if something niggled us. But then it was soon forgotten. When it came to politics and religion it always provoked healthy argument, but usually Graham would save that for his cronies down at the pub. I knew he never stopped loving me.'

'Of course he loved you.'

'See that bureau in the corner over there?' Aunt Agatha pointed to the far wall.

'He made that cabinet for my 25th wedding anniversary. Must have taken him as long as that to make it.
There's oak and mahogany, rosewood and willow, and the marquetry is in satinwood. He used many other woods too but I can't remember them all. My memory must be failing me.'

'I was only admiring it the other morning while doing the dusting. It's a work of art. I've never seen anything like it before.'

'And you are not likely to either. There's only the one. Unique in design. Graham made it in his workshop at the end of the garden. He loved working with wood and you can tell he was a master craftsman by simply looking at that piece. You can say that cabinet is his legacy to the world. He said never to varnish it but wipe it gently with beeswax. I think the satinwood came from Ceylon, the teak from Burma and the mahogany from Malaya. I know for certain the rosewood came from Britain.

'I'm sorry I never got to meet Uncle Graham.'

'He was such a character. It was the Irish in him. Hadn't changed from the first day I saw him in Bloomsbury fixing that blooming door. So was your grandpa, but in a totally different way. As a parson he had great empathy for the poor people who scrabbled around for scraps in the slums of Hackney. There was much poverty in those days even though Victorian history always lauded the might of the empire, and its wealthy inhabitants. Nobody wrote about the poor, or the slums. The rich and the politicians shut their eyes to all that. Someone said "there are the haves and the have nots in this world, and if there's great wealth to be seen there will be even greater poverty not far away. The rich get richer and the poor get poorer."

'Your grandpa encouraged me to read the Bible. He said the greatest stories of all time would be found in it. From love and infidelity, thieving and murder, feats of bravery and charitable acts, treachery and deceit. He said every aspect of life is to be found in the Bible. I read it like I would read an interesting book.'

Through Aunt Agatha, Penny got to understand some of her past. Insights into certain aspects of her early childhood, which if she had not have travelled to Australia she would never have known about. She also discovered some of her rather complex family history.

'This young man you keep getting letters from,' Aunt Agatha spoke, looking curiously at Penny, 'appears to be quite infatuated with you by the way you talk about him. Will he make you a good husband? What I mean is will he be able to support a wife and children? You have to consider these things before you get too involved with someone you only saw so briefly. You don't know the man or what sort of person he might be. You know what I mean. He could be a complete rotter for all you know.'

'He could be a rotter as you say, but my womanly instincts tell me otherwise. In that short time I could tell he was a sensitive person and as lonely as me. He didn't come across as a man who would beat women if that is what's worrying you. As for supporting a wife and children I don't think that will pose any problems. He owns a tea plantation and you know how much tea costs,'

'Fair enough, a good enough reason but are you in love with him?'

'I don't think I can answer that question. I honestly don't know. I'm fond of him and he says he wants to share his life with me. Perhaps what I feel is sympathy for his lonely existence. Whether he will be a good husband or a bad one I could not tell you until after the event. Love can turn to hate and nothing can be guaranteed. Can we be sure of anything? The dividing line is so thin.'

'At least you have given this matter much thought.'

'I have indeed.'

'Has he proposed to you yet?'

'No.'

'But if he asked you to marry him, would you?'

'I might. He is a kindred spirit like me. He and I seem to be in the same boat, cast adrift in the ocean of life.'

'Good repartee. It's your life and you must make the decisions and choose how to live it when you have done so. My only concern is for your happiness, dear.'

'I know you want the best for me, Auntie, and I appreciate your concern for my welfare.'

'You are a very attractive woman and can have any man you want, but more importantly, you need love and to love in your own right. Ceylon is a small country in the middle of nowhere. I know nothing about it but Australia is a big vibrant country, rich and clean with ample scope to develop and thrive. A good place to settle down and raise a family. Australia is so much better than the old country. I'm sure there are plenty of red-blooded men here who would be proud to have you as a wife. You cannot afford to wait too long, dear.'

'I know.'

'Time and tide waits for no man, or woman.'

'I know, but I want to be sure.'

'Nowadays the young call it a mistake when things go wrong. They give up too easily. Sacrifices have to be made. There has to be give and take. I think the correct word is consideration for each other. If there is love, then that is a special gift from God.'

'The world has moved on, Auntie, and we no longer live in Victorian times. We don't need to rush.'

'Life never was a bed of roses to me as a girl. My decision was rushed but I was lucky. I know of some who were not as lucky as me.'

'If Philip asks me to marry him I might just do that. He comes across as a gentle, sensitive and kind man. In the few hours I was in his company, I felt very comfortable.'

'You could grow to love him in time. I've seen that happen many times. You'd be surprised at how funny life can be at times, especially if you have lived as long as I have, my girl.'

'I came out here to keep you company, Auntie, but all this talk about getting married makes me think you want to get rid of me. Am I getting in your way?'

'Nonsense young lady. What on earth gave you this silly idea? Tell me more about your young man from the wilds of Ceylon.'

'Well, he is not my young man. Well, not yet and he is not young. He is 20 years older than me. He is slim, tall, has blue eyes and dark hair, and wears spectacles. By his looks, I mistook him to be a scientist or an explorer. Some might describe him as being handsome.'

'That's a good start. I'm listening. Some might describe him as handsome,' mimicked Aunt Agatha. 'You've told me all I need to know, young lady. You fancy him, don't you?'

'You are incorrigible, Auntie. If you must know I do fancy him. I find Philip Webster very attractive. There is something about him that makes my toes curl. I have many friends in Sydney, both men and women, and I have been escorted to social events by some very handsome men here, but none have had the same effect as Philip on me. There, I have said it now.'

'Good, I think he is the man for you, Penny dear. Please don't feel obliged to turn down his proposal because of me or anything I might have said. Remember, I have lived my life to the full and you are just starting yours. Soon I'll be departing this world and my Graham will be waiting for me.'

The correspondence between Philip and Penny had started on a friendly note but now it had developed into something much deeper and more intimate. Penny was aware of the gradual change and went along with it, though she did not feel quite as strongly as Philip did or express her feelings as ardently as he did. But this form of communication was pleasurable to both. It was obvious to Penny that Philip had fallen in love with her, a love he could no longer contain within himself.

On returning from her brief stay with her aunt, Penny entered her apartment to find another letter from Philip waiting for her. He had written asking her to marry him right away. He needed her badly. Penny wrote back saying it was an important decision to make that would change both their lives forever. She needed time to think. She valued her aunt's views. She also had to sort out her commitments to her employers. She promised to write to him as soon as she was able to resolve these matters.

Penny had already made up her mind to marry Philip. Mrs Penny Webster had a nice ring to it she thought. But she would not break the news to anyone before she told her aunt.

With this uppermost in her mind, she visited her aunt the following day which happened to be Sunday. It was a beautiful day with the sun blazing down from a cloudless sky. She hadn't felt as happy in a long time. Aunt Agatha had voiced her opinions many times and each time the theme was of marriage. However attractive her niece was, her good looks would fade in time. She had to find a suitable partner and settle down. Her aunt had said so, quite bluntly, many times. If not Philip then some nice young Australian.

'Hello, Auntie. What an absolutely gorgeous day.' Penny greeted Aunt Agatha having gone in through the side entrance, dodging the climbing rose that needed tying back.

'Hello, Penny dear, you seem to be in high spirits,' Aunt Agatha saw the excitement in Penny's flushed face.

'I was just about to put the kettle on. Your timing is perfect. I bet you could do with nice cup of tea. Why don't you go into the front room and make yourself comfortable, I won't be long.'

Penny followed her aunt into the kitchen instead of going into the front room. 'I have some great news for you.'

'I can see that by the way your face is flushed. You can tell me all about it in good time, as soon as I have made us some tea. Then we can sit down comfortably and we can talk.'

Making tea seemed to take forever as she watched her aunt get some biscuits from the big tin on the shelf above the cooker and set the tea tray in readiness. As soon as everything was ready Penny carried the tea tray into the front room and set it on the table next to where her aunt usually sat.

Aunt Agatha was the first to speak. 'I can see you are bursting with impatience to tell me your good news. I can tell it's good news by the excitement in your eyes. Come on, dear, don't keep me in suspense any longer.'

Penny sat down in the chair that was Uncle Graham's favourite and drew a long breath to calm the excitement she felt. 'Philip has finally asked me to marry him,' she was glad her news was out at last. She had not told anyone until now.

'I guessed it was something like that, dear.'

'Was I that transparent?'

'So Philip finally managed to summon up the courage to ask you. Congratulations, Penny dear.'

'Thank you, Auntie.'

'Have you accepted his offer?'

'Well, not yet. I wrote to him saying I had to have your approval first. After all, you are the only family I have and I value your thoughts on the subject.'

'Ah, Penny, you are dear girl, and very close to my heart but whatever I have to say or have said in the past must not cloud your feelings for this man. This has to your decision alone. The time to be positive has come. I know you like this man very much but I don't think you are in love with him. That is my view, but that should not matter a jot whether I'm right or wrong. This is your future we are talking about. You told me he loves you, and you find him attractive, caring and sensitive. Being in love is important but not *that* important. Respect is very important. In time you may grow to love him as much as he loves you.

'I've heard in certain parts of the world marriages are arranged and the bride only gets to see her husband for the very first time on her wedding day. I'm told these marriages do work out well and are more stable and longer-lasting than those in our society. Don't get me wrong. What's good for them is not necessarily good for us. Probably their customs may have something to do with dowries and such things that don't concern us.' Aunt Agatha paused, looking at Penny in a whimsical manner.

'You have no dowry for your new husband, have you? Well, not until I die, and what I have is not a lot.'

'I know that one can be misled by the words in letters especially if it comes from a lonely person. At least one thing I do know is that he is not after my wealth.' Penny laughed and her aunt joined in. 'He knows I do not have money.'

'On a serious note,' Aunt Agatha said, pouring each a cup of tea, 'being a married woman gives that special status single women envy. A sense of emotional security. To have a man to depend on, and be loved and cherished, and to be cared for, unlike an unmarried woman. I don't like the word spinster. Sounds too Victorian with all the images that brings to mind. A sort of social stigma. In those days spinsters were dependent on the family, or some charity, or going from one job to another trying to glean a livelihood. Most of the spinsters I knew were unpaid housekeepers in return for a roof over their heads. Others looked after aged parents or relatives. Spinster is not a nice word.'

'I must admit it sounds ghastly. To think I was heading in that direction.'

'Also you can have children, whereas spinsters are ostracised by society whatever their station in life.'

'True, I am illegitimate and I have paid my pound of flesh to society.'

'You will accept won't you?'

'Do I have your approval?'

'I see no reason to disapprove, dear.'

'I will accept then. I think I am doing the right thing.'

'I think you are my dear.'

'I feel so much better talking with you.'

'That is what relatives are for. Giving moral support and strength when needed. Will you be marrying Philip in Ceylon? My personal view on this is that your wedding should take place here. There is so much more dignity in the man coming to the woman than the woman presenting herself to the man, so to speak.'

'Oh, there is no question of me going to him. If he loves me and wants me as much as he says he does, he will come here. Philip is a gentleman. He will marry me here. Besides, I want him to meet you.'

'I am pleased for you, Penny dear. You have taken a huge weight off my mind. If there is anything I can do for you, or I should say, for the both of you, please let me know.'

'Thank you, Auntie. Your approval was all I wanted. I am going to miss you terribly.' There were tears in Penny's eyes.

'I will miss you too, dear. But such is life and life must continue ad infinitum.'

When Penny left her aunt's bungalow later that evening, the only cloud on the horizon was the thought of leaving a frail old lady to fend for herself in Sydney while she went to live with her new husband in Ceylon. Despite her aunt's resilience to the rigours of old age and her fierce defence of her independence, Penny knew in her heart that she would never see her aunt again once she left Australia.

Penny wrote to Philip accepting his proposal of marriage. Philip telegraphed her back to say he was leaving Colombo on the first available steamer. Penny's contract with St Matthew's School for Girls was due for renewal, as the governors had decided to keep her on for another year but when she told them she was getting married and would be leaving for Ceylon they expressed their regrets. They were sorry to see her leave and wished her well for the future.

The wedding itself was a simple ceremony with Aunt Agatha and a few of Penny's friends being present. Both Penny and Philip preferred it that way, and left Australia the following day on their honeymoon cruise back to Ceylon.

CHAPTER SIX

The sun was streaming through the chinks in the curtains when Penny awoke from a deep sleep.

It was late morning. She stretched herself like a cat with her eyes still closed and put out a hand expecting Charlie to be lying next to her. Then she remembered Charlie had left in the early hours of that morning. The events of the previous evening came sharply into focus as she lay there. She opened her eyes, adjusted her pillows, and sat up in bed. She was relaxed and at ease with herself. All the tensions of the previous few months had miraculously vanished. She was a woman satisfied. A woman invigorated again. A woman who was whole again.

Presently she got out of bed, pulled the curtains open and then went back to bed to savour the events of the night. She had not quite planned to do the things that happened. It just happened. She was carried away by the atmosphere of the moment, her own demanding needs, and the attention of a virile young man who found her attractive. What had started as mere flirting escalated and she was unable to stop. If she was truthful, she did not want it to stop. She was desperate to snap out of the dull and dreary rut that she had fallen into since her husband became unable to fulfil her needs.

Charlie was young and refreshingly inexperienced in his love making, but that was to be expected from a man who had not made love to a woman before. His haste and clumsiness added an extra spice. With guidance and patience, and taking the initiative when necessary, the next time would be better and the time after that better still. Charlie was an eager learner and it was so natural to guide him.

Waiting for Tuesday to come seemed to take forever but the new lovers were able to keep their tryst as arranged, at the Grand Hotel. Charlie watched from the foyer as Penny came in, collected her key, and went up the stairs as casually as she could without looking around. If she saw Charlie she ignored him. But as soon as the coast was clear Charlie sneaked into her room unnoticed.

To him the casual fling with Penny had already developed into something much stronger. Charlie had fallen in love with Penny Webster. In spite of her resolutions, Penny too found herself being drawn into their clandestine affair. She found it impossible to keep away from Charlie.

Meeting as discreetly as possible, each tryst was short and hurried for fear that their illicit affair would sooner or later become public knowledge. The two met whenever they could. Sometimes to play tennis or to swim with friends to keep up appearances. Other times at remote beauty spots to kiss and cuddle and spend some time with each other. They met whenever or wherever they could, even though it was always not possible for them to make love.

They were playing with fire but the dangers also flamed their passions more intensely. Charlie was prone to recklessness. He was in love and he could not care less if the whole world knew, but Penny knew that if their small community found out, she would be ostracised and pilloried as a loose woman. A married woman almost twice the age of her young lover. Seducing the son of a prominent and respected family. To Charlie, staying away from Penny was torture and Penny needed him as she had never needed a man.

As usual, they were exposed when they took one chance too many.

On his return from Colombo, Philip was pleased to see that his wife had cast aside the cloak of depression that had shrouded their lives in recent months. Penny was alive and cheerful again and entertaining their friends at Kandalami. They had begun to portray themselves as a happily married couple who had recovered from the sticky patch that most marriages go through from time to time.

Penny was radiating all the confidence of the earlier years and she was back to her social best. Philip was relieved that matters had been resolved. Seeing his wife so cheerful was pleasing. He had come to accept this as perhaps another phase of their lives. The household at Kandalami had settled once again into its normal routines.

But about three weeks had passed since Charlie and Penny were able to make love and the strain made them take one risk too many. Like fireflies bouncing off lanterns in the night, it was inevitable their wings would get burned.

It was arranged that Penny, Clara and Kylie would go shopping while Philip and James, Charlie's father, played a round of golf at the exclusive Mile High Club at Nuwara Eliya, so named because it was one mile above sea level.

'Let's play for fun. Why spoil a good day in these beautiful surroundings. Stick a wager on and the game takes on a different complexion. Our animal competitiveness kicks in and what could be a pleasant past-time inevitably changes into a battle of contention.'

'Okay by me, Philip. How are things at Kandalami?'

'Fine, but that cannot be said for Britain. We are getting an almighty battering from the Nazis. I hear many parts of London and the South East, Coventry, Manchester and Liverpool and many other cities and towns have been reduced to rubble by the nightly bombing with heavy loss of lives. I read in one newspaper that we are using empty swimming pools to store the dead until they could be buried. A pretty dreadful business but we must take our hats off to Churchill. He will fight on like the bulldog he is, but we do need the Americans. If they don't help us, the Nazis will be putting up their tents in the royal parks before long.'

'We need the Canadians, the Australians, the Indians, and every man jack from the Empire if we are going to beat Hitler. Personally, I blame Chamberlain. He had enough time to read the signs. He knew what was on the cards but stuck his head in the sand. We should have been better prepared. The French were supposed to put up a better show but they folded up so dismally.'

'Stalin is sitting on the fence and Mussolini is hedging his bets but we can count on Churchill. He will give Hitler a bloody nose. You tee off.'

'I have upped production. Don't forget tea is an essential commodity.'

'I think we all have. I've got Charlie working his balls off at Glencoe.'

'We can do the best we can. Every little helps.'

The men played in silence for a while.

'Do you get much bother from the wild animals behind your house? It never ceases to amaze me, even now, at how well you have established yourself on the edge of that mountain.'

'The animals are no problem but we could do with fewer snakes. Clara and Kylie hate snakes. That and those creepy crawlies.'

'I know Penny can't stand them either. Your fence must get breached from time to time. Do you have to kill any of those dangerous animals that wander in?'

'A few shots in the air seems to do the trick. I made a resolution many years ago not to kill anything for the sheer thrill of killing. These animals are such wonderful creatures. That is what attracted me here in the first instance. If you live in a country with such a diversity of wildlife it is daft to then go and destroy them, whatever the reason. Killing animals just to acquire a trophy to hang on the wall or have stuffed to me is an evil act. Aren't we all God's creatures too? Rupert and Kylie never had the urge to wander into the wild but Charlie is different. He can track animals by their footprints and gauge how close they are by the freshness of their droppings. He can tell the age of a leopard by the size of their pug marks.'

'How extraordinary. It has been claimed that when Adam was cast out of the Garden of Eden he came to this island and when he died he was buried on the mountain that is now called Adam's Peak.'

'I would not argue with that theory. This is the Garden of Eden as far as I'm concerned but I bloody well wish he had not brought those serpents with him.'

'Very droll, James,' laughed Philip missing his six-foot putt.

'Temptations of the flesh never come cheap,' replied James sinking in his putt. 'There is always a price attached to the sins we commit. Eve did not get off lightly when she succumbed to the delights of the forbidden fruit either.'

'Neither was the Garden of Eden ever the same again. The next hole is a par four and I have never been able to make par yet.'

'I try to keep to the right of the fairway and let the wind do the work.'

James teed off from the tenth. 'Damn, I screwed my shot. I think I'm in the rough. I'll be lucky to get down in six.'

Philip teed off and found the fairway but was about 30 yards behind James.

'I think I should use a wedge and hack it back onto the fairway,' James looked enquiringly at his caddy. 'What do you advise?'

'A sand wedge might help but the three bunkers further up could be a problem.'

'My options are limited. A wedge it is.'

The two tea planters finished their round of 18 holes.

'Thank you for a splendid game, old chap. I'm ready for lunch.'

'I'm ready for a stiff whisky and soda. I expect the ladies have had fun too.'

Later the men were having their drinks in the club house when the ladies returned from the shops, but Penny was not with them.

'Hello, Philip, James, good game was it?' enquired Clara, giving James a peck on his cheek. 'All this shopping has given me an appetite. Penny would have been in her element but unfortunately she had to cry off saying she had a headache. She went back to the Grand. I don't think it was anything to worry about. Just one of those things. She wanted to be excused from lunch and said she will see you later.'

'Hello, Clara. Hello, Kylie. I lost as usual. Your husband should take up golf professionally.'

'Nonsense, old boy, the Gods were smiling on me today. The ladies in our lives are exceedingly pretty. I can see why we indulge them with their every wish.'

'But of course, James. No point in being surrounded by pretty ladies and not doing so. I expect you cannot refuse Clara any of her demands.'

'Thank you for your compliments,' Clara smiled sweetly looking pleased.

'And two fine upstanding sons,' continued Philip, 'and a beautiful daughter to be proud of.'

'Why thank you, kind sir,' smiled Kylie. 'You don't do so badly yourself. Penny is the life and soul at parties, and she is stunningly beautiful. But then I'm not telling you something you don't already know. Where have you been hiding yourself recently?'

'Oh, you know I'm not one for parties. That is Penny's scene and I go along to please her. Still, it keeps her out of mischief. I think I will pop in and see how she is rather than holding you up. Why don't you go ahead. We can make lunch another time.'

'Philip, another whisky before you go?'

'I cannot think of any good reason not to. Thank you.'

After more small talk, Philip finished his drink and went to see how Penny was getting on.

The Grand Hotel was busier than usual when Philip walked in. Penny was nowhere to be seen in the reception area that fanned off from the foyer so he headed to the stairs that took him to their room. On opening the door he expected to see his wife in bed. She was, but so was a man with her. And they were making passionate love. To his amazement and shock, Philip recognised the man who was making love to his wife as none other than Charlie Digby-Sloan, his golfing partner's son.

Penny was the first to see Philip, and she froze, her heart turning to ice.

'What the hell—' Charlie exclaimed as he turned round and saw Philip framed in the doorway, the words choking in his throat. There was nothing he could do as he lay there, as did Penny.

Philip looked at his wife dumbstruck, then glared at Charlie. No one uttered a word for what appeared to be an eternity until Penny broke the silence.

'I'm sorry, Charlie. It is best you left now. Please go.'

'But—'

'Don't say anything, Charlie. Please go.'

Charlie scrambled out of the bed and scurried into the bathroom. Philip glared at his wife, then turned and stormed out of the room, slamming the door shut after him and retraced his footsteps towards the bar and ordered a large whisky and soda.

Charlie got dressed hurriedly. 'Bloody hell, that was Philip. Why did you not tell me he was here with you?'

'I'm sorry Charlie. Philip and your father were out playing golf and it presented us with the chance to be together. I was meant to join Clara, Kylie, your father and Philip for lunch. But I lied to them saying I was feeling unwell so that we could see each other. I was desperate to see you, Charlie. I did not expect Philip to come here looking for me. Let's be calm and think rationally. I think you had better go now. I will sort this out. Use the side exit. Leave Philip to me. Do not breathe a word of this to anyone. Understand? Go now. I am truly sorry this has happened. This was my fault entirely.'

'We are both to blame. Don't worry, I won't desert you. They would have found out about us sooner rather than later.'

'Hush, leave this to me. Not another word, please. Please go now, Charlie,' implored Penny.

With a last glance at Penny, Charlie left the room closing the door behind him silently.

Penny knew her husband too well after so many years of marriage. Philip hated public displays of emotion, or for that matter, confrontations that could be embarrassing. She knew he would be hurting badly and utterly humiliated but she also knew he would not scream and shout and have a terrible row. He would pull the shutters around him, bottle up his emotions, get withdrawn and sulk, and lose himself in whisky. She also knew where to find him. He would be quietly getting himself blind-drunk at the bar.

By the time Penny had gone down her husband had downed a few whiskies.

'You better check us out,' Penny spoke to her husband as if nothing untoward had happened. 'I will wait for you in the car. It is time we went home, don't you think?'

Philip said nothing but looked at her like a wounded family pet, then looked at his empty glass.

'I will drive us home if that is all right with you.'

Philip said not one word.

'I will wait for you in the car.' Penny sensed it was not the time or the place for words. She knew all that would come later. Much later. All she could do was wait until her husband was ready to leave the bar.

She had a long wait before Philip came out of the hotel worse for wear and got into the seat next to her. They drove home in silence.

While the men buried what was left of their compatriots Charlie scouted the outer perimeter of the drop zone. He had no difficulties in finding the trail the Japanese soldiers had taken with their plunder. It appeared they had not made any effort to cover their tracks. They were confident there were no allied troops in the vicinity and were careless. He saw from their boot prints, flattened grass and cigarette butts. The enemy had been waiting for some time for the British soldiers who were killed as they came down in their parachutes. He guessed they must have cracked into the wireless signals being sent out. If Scottie's wireless had been working they too would have been killed by now.

Now those same boot prints and broken scrub would make it easy to track them. The evidence told Charlie that rain had not fallen in the past two days. But there was need to go after them fast. They had to get them before they reached their main camp. The Japs were headed in a north-easterly direction.

Charlie reported his findings to Captain Lee who ordered his men to move out after he was satisfied that every British soldier killed was in a makeshift grave of some kind. The weight of the supplies the enemy had plundered would have slowed the Japs down.

When the commandos did catch up with the raiding party, they saw the enemy had bivouacked for the night on an open patch of grassland that commanded a clear view of the surrounding area. But they had become less vigilant. The sentries looked bored and relaxed. Assessing the situation from the edge of the jungle, Captain Lee knew he had to cross that open ground without being seen or be cut down by enemy fire. With his depleted team, the element of surprise and good fortune would be needed if they were to be successful.

From the size of their camp he estimated the enemy to be between 20 or 30 but he had decided he would take them on. Visibility was good. After much deliberation he decided he would mount his attack at dawn and withdrew back into the dense vegetation to map out a strategy.

None of the men had much sleep that night and they were eager to get on with the job. The plan was to crawl through the thick grass and get as close to the enemy as possible under cover of darkness. The sentries would be dispatched first, silently. Then lob a few grenades, followed by rapid fire, and finally a bayonet attack.

An hour before daybreak, Captain Lee deployed his men as prearranged. When the signal was given, three men crept up to the sleeping sentries, put one hand over their mouths, sank their bayonets into their bodies, twisted, and then out. The execution was neat, professional and completed with the minimum of fuss and was over in seconds. The rest, who were still stirring from their slumber were destroyed before the enemy had a chance to draw their weapons. The plan had worked to perfection. All were killed with no loss to his own men.

They retrieved all the supplies that were left including those of the dead, and more importantly they had the high explosives and detonators they needed for the next phase of their mission. They took all the ammunition and guns they could carry. The rest were carried into the jungle and buried in waterproof coverings for later use.

Two hours later Captain Lee gave the order to press forward towards their next objective. Blowing up roads, communication lines and fuel dumps. But before they could get on with this, the monsoons had started in earnest. Heavy torrential rain had turned many parts of the rainforest into something akin to a swamp. Coping with the wet and humid conditions with their heavy packs was a daily nightmare. The constant battles with mosquitoes and leeches added to their problems as did their daily squelch in wet clothes and boots.

So far none had gone down with malaria or any other tropical diseases despite the conditions they endured. On the third day of constant rain they came across what looked like a small, abandoned hamlet. To continue to press forward in these conditions was madness and Captain Lee gave the order that they would rest there for a couple of days in the makeshift huts to dry out and recuperate. As a fighting force his men were useless. It was a risk. There was no alternative.

The two days' rest worked wonders and morale was high. The risk had paid off. But the order to move was given again. Get their heavy packs on and shamble back into the jungle to face the unknown, and the constant irritation from the swarms of insects the rains had brought to life and lay in wait for their blood. Little streams had turned into raging silt-carrying rivers which made crossing them extremely hazardous and dangerous. But with sheer doggedness, Captain Lee urged his men on until it became abundantly clear he and his men were at breaking point.

'Charlie we need to hole up again until this beastly weather eases. What do you think?'

'The men are exhausted, sir, and we are not making any progress whatsoever but more important is our supplies. If our ammo and explosives deteriorate we might as well turn around and head for the coast.'

'My thoughts exactly. Can you keep your eyes peeled for a suitable place?'

'We skirted some huge boulders by that fast-flowing river yesterday. It would make an ideal place if we can find some caves. We can keep our supplies and ourselves dry. By camouflaging ourselves into the surroundings, the enemy will never find us, unless of course, we get careless. The elevation from those boulders will give us good vantage points and enough time to make ourselves invisible. Also we will have a good supply of fresh water.'

'Brilliant. Let's go find those caves, men.'

After discarding several caves, Charlie found the one he was looking for. It was big and airy and large enough for eight men and all their supplies. Moreover, it was on high ground about 30 yards from the river and it had several openings.

Charlie took charge of operations. First he had to check the cave for snakes, scorpions, centipedes, monitor lizards, ants' nests and other jungle inhabitants that may have taken up residence there. His next task was to try and find some dry kindling which seemed to be a tall order considering the wet weather but he knew where to look and soon made two flaming torches and burned out any unwanted pests and debris. The roof of the cave was high enough to have a fire at night, which kept out insects and animals from wandering in and the mosquitoes at bay.

Thanks to Charlie, the men had a cosy cave to sit out the monsoon. He was also able to demonstrate his amazing survival skills. The use of a small magnifying glass to ignite dry leaves when the sun shone, or the use of shaving mirrors to signal to each other, or catching fish with pointed and barbed bamboo rods and baking them in pits of glowing charcoals, or trapping game to grill or slowly roast on an open spit. Their cave was large enough to do all this and these were skills he had learned as a schoolboy and tested in the jungles of Ceylon.

There was an abundance of fresh fruits, vegetables and edible roots and yams to eat. They had fresh water to drink, to wash their clothes and to bath. Life had taken on a completely different meaning as they sat out the heavy intermittent downpours.

But Captain Lee was always aware of the dangers the enemy posed and sentries were posted day and night. From the many vantage points around them they could find no trace of the Japs. Neither were there any sightings of the indigenous people of the land. Captain Lee had ordered his men to avoid being seen by the natives and they took measures to detour around any settlements they saw.

Time stood still for a few months but the monsoon weather stopped as quickly as it had started and with it came the end of their idyllic sojourn from the realities of war after sighting that enemy activity in their area had started again. Soon the order to vacate their cave it came shortly before noon on a blistering hot and humid day. After making sure they had obliterated all signs of their occupation, they pressed on back into the jungle.

CHAPTER SEVEN

The plane droned through the moonlit night cutting through the few clouds on its way to Burma. The heavily camouflaged special commandos knew that the time would soon arrive for them to float down into the jungle below not knowing what to expect. Charlie closed his eyes but sleep eluded him, his mind in turmoil, trying to imagine what awaited him. Whether he survived the rigours of the jungle or the enemy waiting to be engaged was something he tried to put out of his mind. He wished the tightness in the pit of his stomach would go away.

In the dim light that came in from the portholes he could hardly see the faces of the men beside him but he could feel their tenseness. Nervous and apprehensive like him. That was except for Captain Robert Lee. He was slumped on his side next to Charlie but he could not see if his commander was asleep or pretending to be asleep. Charlie knew the mission ahead would be tough. He knew he could cope with the jungle but in this jungle there were humans waiting to kill him and he would have to kill many to stay alive.

He switched his mind to Penny and imagined he was walking hand in hand with her on the silvery sand of Mount Lavinia beach, the engine drone the sound of the breaking waves on the reef. But his reverie was suddenly broken by the pilot who announced they would reach their drop zone in approximately 12 minutes, 1 hour and 20 minutes before dawn.

Silently they took their places ready to bail out when the signal came. Charlie was the third out of the plane and landed in heavy scrub. Luck was on their side and they all landed with no injuries, but there one major accident that was crucial to their operation. They did not know that the radio transmitter was badly damaged until a little later.

Crawfie had drifted furthest and was tangled in a tree but they cut him down quickly. If the Japs had spotted their plane and watched them drifting down there were no signs of a reception party waiting to pick them off.

The men went about their business silently and efficiently. Parachutes were buried and their supplies gathered and they were ready to defend themselves in case of an attack. 'Got everything, men? Let's get some cover,' ordered Captain Lee.

'Sir, the wireless is busted,' reported Scottie their communications man. 'The huge dent suggests it caught a rock.'

'Blast.' Captain Lee sounded exasperated. 'We need that equipment. Get it fixed as soon as you can Scottie.'

On Captain Lee's order, the men moved out cautiously deeper into the scrub and waited for the first rays of light to come through the gaps in the branches about half a mile from where they had landed. The day promised to be sunny. After checking his compass and map Captain Lee pointed the direction they were to take. The only sounds around them came from the insects, birds, and small creatures that protested vociferously at their presence. What they saw around them was strange. Unreal, and foreboding.

The first day saw the commandos make heavy work as they hacked their way through thick, dense vegetation, stopping for short breaks. Progress was slow. With an hour to sunset the order was given to find a suitable place to camp for the night. Their first day on Burmese soil was uneventful but the baptism of the heat and humidity, flies and insects, was unlike anything they had trained for on the bleak expanses of Dartmoor.

The next day was sunny too and they were to get their first glimpse of the enemy. The men had moved out from their overnight bivouac an hour after sunrise but their progress was no faster than the previous day as they hacked their way through the brush. They were about to have another short break when they stumbled on what looked like an overgrown, narrow, disused track, and were debating to see where it led when suddenly they heard voices up ahead.

They had barely enough time to take cover when a patrol of eight soldiers went past only a few yards from where they were crouched. The Japs felt safe because they were laughing and jabbering as they went by. Captain Lee had signalled his men not to attack.

'We could have taken them out, sir. They were so close,' whispered George.

'Too bloody close for comfort, if you ask me,' replied John in a hoarse whisper.

'We could have,' replied Captain Lee softly, 'but my guess is this patrol is from a nearby camp. They were relaxed so that tells us much. If my assumption is correct, there must be a large force nearby. If we had a go we could have taken that patrol out but in doing so we would have given our position away and been wiped out ourselves. Remember our mission men. We only take on the enemy when it suits us. There will be plenty of opportunities for heroics I can assure you. Your eagerness to fight is commendable but to charge in blind is foolhardy. I suggest we reconnoitre the area with great care and see how big the hornets' nest is first.'

The jungle track they had stumbled on was one of many that radiated out from a large camp about four miles east of them. If the Japs got wind of them, the enemy would not have taken long to find and destroy them. Captain Lee's esteem as an astute leader went up by several degrees in the eyes of his men. He was to reinforce this further a week later.

Hacking their way through dense vegetation was slow and energy sapping in the sweltering heat. The oppressive climate was slowing them down and beginning to take its toll on his men and they needed to get away from an area of much enemy activity. There was no other way but to gamble and take one of the tracks and take their chances in dodging the patrols that used them.

Two men were deployed ahead of the main group to act as scouts and trail blazers. Captain Lee reasoned it was the best way forward if his men were to progress and reach their next drop zone. Any movement at night was out due to the inhospitality of the area and the treacherous terrain. The plan worked and they put some distance between themselves and the Jap encampment. But the jungle paths had come to an end and their progress was slowed down again.

One week had passed since they had landed on Burmese soil. On the eight day, an early start was made under overcast skies but after toiling for about two hours without much progress Captain Lee ordered his exhausted men to take a break in what appeared to be a dried up river bed.

Charlie and Scottie were assigned to sentry duty. Charlie positioned himself at the highest point that commanded a good view of the area behind them, while Scottie covered their forward route.

Over the short time they were in the jungle, his commander and his men observed Charlie's natural affinity to his surroundings. They watched him with interest as he read and understood the signs that went unnoticed to the others. A newly broken branch; fresh leaves and green twigs on the ground; the sudden flight of birds; the anguished screams of monkeys; or the excited shrill of the squirrels had a special significance to Charlie. Skills he had learned in the jungles of Ceylon as a boy. He watched for snakes and other reptiles which liked to sun themselves in open patches of ground soon after sunrise. He knew where there would be the most leeches in the rainy season. He watched and listened to his father and the natives on their expeditions into the more dangerous regions of his native country. Soon Captain Lee came to rely on Charlie for his jungle craft and sought his views before deciding what manoeuvres to make.

The men had gratefully settled for a well-deserved rest when Charlie hurried down from his position, looked for his commander and found him. 'Sir, I think we have company. I think the enemy have found us. They know we are here and have been trailing us.'

'What makes you think so?'

'Did you notice those monkeys over there?' Charlie pointed to some tall trees in the distance.

'Can't say that I did.'

'Something frightened those monkeys and made them scatter fast. It had to be a big animal for them to react like that. A snake would make them scream and jump about from a safe distance if threatened to alert the rest of the troupe. Also a flock of birds took flight fast close to where those monkeys were.'

'Distance, Charlie?'

'I'd guess, maybe one to two hundred yards. Not more.'

'Let's see if your hunch is correct. Quick. Take cover. You,' he pointed to Maake and Crawfie, 'drop back. The rest of you take the flanks and find whatever cover you can. Select your targets and wait for my signal. When I raise my hand, fire at will. You know the drill. Then go in with your bayonets. No prisoners. Be snappy.'

They needed combat experience if this mission was to go anywhere and this was the ideal situation to blood his men. The conditions were as good as any he could have picked to get to grips with the enemy. No matter how much training his men had had, there was no substitute for the real thing. He needed to see how his men fared in actual combat. There was no other way if the enemy had their sights on them. Be the hunters and not the hunted.

He watched his men move quickly and silently. Each knew what was expected of him. After ascertaining that all was to his satisfaction he took cover where he would be the first to see the Japs when they came into sight. The ambush was set.

The waiting seemed an eternity. Charlie's throat was as dry as the river bed he was standing in. He was conscious that he would look very foolish if his reading of the signs came to nothing. A few monkeys cavorting. What a flipping joke. His mates would have a field day. From his position he could see two of his comrades. They were tense, straining their eyes to catch a glimpse of the Japs, or rubbing the palms of their hands on their uniforms to get rid of the clamminess, or wiping the sweat from getting into their eyes.

Suddenly he saw a Jap, then two, moving rapidly and silently in a crouched position, darting in and out of the sparse vegetation and rocks as they came towards them. Then he saw more. There was no laughter or banter this time. They were searching for their quarry. He was extremely relieved that he had read the signs correctly.

Charlie counted 15 men in khaki, heavily camouflaged, but he guessed there were more searching for them to frighten those monkeys and birds. If he had not trusted his instincts they could have been in that ambush instead of the Jap fighters.

The minutes dragged on. Charlie hoped none of his mates had left behind any signs to alert the Japs. The ambush was hurriedly set up and the element of surprise was on their side but if they had left any signs it was too late to do much about it.

The enemy was almost upsides of them. Still, no signal from their leader. They waited with bated breath. Just as Charlie thought the attack had been aborted, the signal was given. The sudden noise of gunfire broke the stillness of the jungle. Charlie saw the twisted faces of the screaming Japs, blood staining their uniforms as they fell. It was unreal.

Like watching a slow-motion film. He fired at two in rapid fire and saw them fall but there were more to his left screaming and charging towards him as bullets whizzed around him, forcing him to drop to the ground and roll behind a boulder. The split second he needed saved him. He drew a quick breath, jumped out and fired again as bullets ricocheted off the boulder. He saw more Japs swarming like hornets, but more Japs fell.

He realised his sub-machine gun was empty but there was no time to reload. He rolled over twice, got up in time into a crouching position and thrust his bayonet into a screaming body which knocked him sideways as he felt his steel blade sink into flesh. He lay there dazed for a moment. He heard much gunfire and saw the soldier he had bayoneted dead next to him. But as swiftly as their attack had begun it was over. Everything had gone silent except for a few groans and a lot of swearing.

'Come on,' barked Captain Lee, his voice echoing around the rocks of the river bed. 'Get on the double. Check all are dead. Come on, get a move on. We don't want any skulking away and giving our position away.' The brisk orders came thick and fast. 'If any of the bastards are still alive, dispatch them swiftly. We take no prisoners.'

After the men had gone about their orders, Captain Lee surveyed the area. 'Have we got them all? Any casualties? Well done, Charlie, you helped to save our bacon today. How many did you get?'

'Don't know, sir. Maybe a few. I saw Maake take a tumble.'

'Check him out will you.'

Later. 'The cunning bastards knew we were here. They will be coming after us now. We were lucky this time. Let's give them a run for their money. Take all the weapons and ammo you can carry and all the grenades you can find. You men acquitted yourselves in the highest traditions of the British Forces. This was a well-executed sortie with no loss of life to any of our team. Brilliant. Charlie, is there anything I need to know?'

'We need to get out of here pretty damn fast. As you know animals can smell blood for miles and they will be here soon enough. Carrion will be circling in the sky too. If there are any Japs nearby they will want to check this out. Also, if their patrol did not report back, they are bound to send a bigger detail to investigate the reason why.'

Captain Lee gave the order to evacuate the area. 'Thank you, Charlie. Let's get the hell out of here.'

Soon it was confirmed that all the enemy were dead and none were able to escape. Maake's injury was a graze to his upper thigh which needed patching. Their war had finally started. All had been blooded. The commandos had acquitted themselves with credit but they knew they would need all their skills to stay one step ahead of the enemy. They had to plan every move meticulously and grab their chances when the odds were slanted in their favour.

Later that evening after doubling their sentries, they found a suitable place to bivouac surrounded by boulders, lit a fire using dry logs, ate their rations and were drinking mugs of tea as Captain Lee discussed the day's events.

'This unforeseen event today has probably delayed us getting to our drop zone but there was nothing we could do about that. If we get better terrain we may be able to make up time tomorrow.'

'Shouldn't we have buried those Japs, sir?' enquired Ade.

'No. You men were exhausted and we had to get the hell out of there in case there were other patrols in the vicinity.'

'Those bodies won't be left there for long,' Charlie stated matter of factly. 'The big cats would have most of them. They can smell blood for miles if the wind is in the right direction and what they leave would be taken care of by the *kabaragoyas*, monitor lizards. They grow to about five feet, or the *thalagoyas,* iguanas that grow to maybe under three feet, or the jackals, or the *kadiyas,* big black ants. These ants are vicious and quite painful and you will know that you have been bitten by the swelling on your body. Then there are the *kakkas,* crows and vultures, left to polish off anything left during daylight hours. A couple of days and all that would be left will only be a few bones and their tattered uniforms.'

'It could have been us.'

'More vigilance and more stealth will be the order of the day.'

CHAPTER EIGHT

'I said I would tell you about your father, Penny dear,' Aunt Agatha had settled in her favourite chair by the fire as they had the previous night. 'Are you ready for what I am about to tell you? Some of it could be very upsetting.'

'Yes, Auntie.'

'Are you sure?'

'Very sure. I have a need to know, good or bad. I have spent most of my life wondering why I was so different to the other children but no one was willing or able to tell me about my early life. These gaps need to be filled. I would be most grateful to hear what you have to say.'

'All right, as I said, we called your father Toby. Toby was still at the orphanage when Graham and I left for Australia. I wrote to the orphanage after we had settled down in Sydney and they wrote back to say Toby had left them and was now living with a family. They told me this was normal practice to make room for new orphans. They gave me the address of this family and I wrote to him as often as I could. Most of my letters went unanswered. The few times he wrote he said he was unhappy and preferred the orphanage but that the orphanage would not take him back. He said that as soon as he was old enough he was going to join the Merchant Navy and if he sailed into Sydney Harbour he would pop in and see us. Soon the letters became few and far between, and after a few years his letters stopped altogether. I did not know where to contact him.'

Aunt Agatha stopped talking. Penny saw from her hands and bent head, she was agitated although all of this happened a long time ago. There were many questions raging through her mind but she held her tongue. The silence seemed to go on for long time. Then Aunt Agatha broke her silence.

'As I said it was a long time ago. Several years after Toby's letters stopped I had a letter from the Maritime Office. They informed me, as next of kin, Toby had perished at sea. Apparently it was one of the worst storms of this century. Many ships went down with the loss of many lives.' she paused again. 'The Maritime Office wanted to know if I wanted the few personal effects that had come into their possession? I wrote back to say I wanted every scrap of information they had. Although Toby was lax at letter writing, he kept a detailed diary. From that and other personal documents I was able to trace you. Penny dear, until then I knew nothing of you. Among his belongings was a leather-bound notebook. In it was your name. Where you were at that time, and the amounts he paid regularly for your upkeep. There were other notes scribbled in that notebook too.

'The name Aggie was mentioned several times. From what I could gather, it appeared that your father had met a girl called Aggie. It could have been Agnes or Agatha like my own name but I never found out which. Details were rather sketchy but from the bits and pieces I was able to piece together your father had formed a relationship with this woman, Agnes, or Aggie. She was your mother and she too had been a housemaid. They were to get married when he returned from his next voyage. But when he put to sea it would appear that he was unaware Aggie was carrying his child.

'As fate would have it his ship was delayed following a catalogue of problems and disasters. By the time he reached

London, Aggie had given birth to you. Things were hard in those days, and none of the big houses would keep a pregnant housemaid. As a result, your mother was thrown onto the streets.

'As she had no means to support you or herself, she had to give you up. She left you well wrapped up on the steps of Thomas Coram House in Brunswick Square not far from where she worked. Until then, I understand, she cared for you as best as she could. I know it would have broken her heart to do what she did, and I know she would have loved you dearly, but she also wanted to make certain that you were well cared for.'

'Did you find out what happened to my mother?'

'No, dear. Your distraught father searched high and low for her when he got back. He was absolutely bereft. He walked the streets of London day and night for weeks looking for Aggie. He checked with the police, the local hospitals, and even the Salvation Army but Aggie had vanished. The police, insensitive to the core, said they fished out several bodies of young women from the Thames every week, usually with no identification. But he eventually found you at Thomas Coram House from the note pinned inside your blanket.'

'So I'm illegitimate.' Penny stated the words as a matter of fact.

'That word means nothing to me, dear. You had a father and a mother. I know in my heart you were loved and wanted. Circumstances beyond their control prevented them from getting married. The world can be so cruel at times. As far as I am concerned you are a gift from God. A precious gift to this world we live in, and such a wonderful gift,' Aunt Agatha stretched out her frail hand and gently placed it on Penny's knee.

'Thank you, Auntie.'

'Nothing to thank me for, dear. If we had known sooner, Graham and I would have had you like a shot, and given you all the love that you missed out on as a child. We would have treated you as our child. In spite of the love Graham and I had for each other, God in His wisdom, did not see fit to bless us with children. I know Graham was disappointed but he never blamed me for it. These things are the will of God, and He may have had His reasons for this.'

Penny was suddenly overcome by emotion. There was nothing she could say. Her throat was dry and the tears streamed down her cheeks. She got out of her chair, went to her aunt, put her arms around her and hugged her. Her aunt too was wrestling with her own emotions. Penny broke away after a while and silently went into her little box room next to the kitchen to seek the solace she needed.

Aunt Agatha never spoke about her father again. The days that followed were spent in the same routine sitting by the fireplace. Light supper, tidying up, retiring to the front room before it was time for bed. Aunt Agatha would persevere with her knitting and Penny with her reading. But sometimes Aunt Agatha would put her knitting down and they would chat.

The day after the ambush, and as darkness fell, the commandos bivouacked in a densely scrubby outcrop by a small river. Sentries were posted on two-hourly shifts, although spotting any patrols would have been impossible in the heavy rain. Captain Lee thought it highly improbable but he was taking no risks. The men had managed to get a fire going and sat solemnly smoking and talking in low voices when he joined them.

'We have been riding our luck but all our training will be for nothing if we get rumbled. What we learned in Dartmoor may help us but not a lot. We need to bone up on jungle lore. We must learn to read and recognise the signs of the wilderness. If we are to outwit the enemy we need to be one step ahead of them. It is a tall order but we must learn quickly if we are to survive. Charlie, I want you to stay close to me.'

'Will do, sir.'

'Have any of you any observations that I should know about since we arrived?'

'If I see anything that you need to know I will bring it to your attention, sir.'

'All I have observed so far is lots of jungle, sir.' Quipped one wise guy to nervous laughter.

'Jolly good.' Captain Lee joined in the laughter. 'I'm going to get some kip, it's going to be a busy day tomorrow.'

The men, however, appeared to be restless.

'I've seen some water buffaloes but I doubt there are any hippos, or lions or giraffes,' Maake was being silly but his attempt at sarcasm was lost on his comrades. 'Quite different to Kenya.'

'Nothing like Darwin either,' Crawfie said. 'I ain't seen any kangaroos but the mosquitoes and insects are real, and I wouldn't put it past you but some of those waterholes could be home to some nasty crocs. Back home the waterholes are full of them. Some have been known to grow up to 30 feet. Man, you've no chance with them. They wait and watch you and then strike like greased lightning.'

'Go on, 30-foot crocs? I don't believe there are any here,' said Scottie working on his wireless set.

'Thank God for that. Should be a walk in the park then, won't it.' John sneered.

'I heard there were crocs as big as that on the beaches of Barbados, ain't that right, George?'

'Yeah, I heard that rumour too,' laughed Freddie.

'Where you been, man, crocs on beaches in Barbados. You gone crazy, or somethin'?' Brandon looked around him in amazement.

'He's having you on, Brandon. The pictures I saw of those animals on the beach had stripes.'

'Well, there are no such things in Barbados or Trinidad. You tell 'em, Elvis.'

'Only beautiful women in wispy bikinis.'

'How come I seen nothing yet?' said Eddie who had dosed off.

'You will Eddie when they grab you by the short and the curlies.' The men fell about with laughter.

The banter went on for a while and then died down. Crawfie lay down next to Charlie. 'Thanks, matie.' There was no mistaking the appreciation in his voice. 'A brilliant piece of sentry duty. I owe you one.'

'Just doing my job, Crawfie. Good shooting. I heard you took out two today.'

'Actually I got three but I'm not one to brag.'

None of the men said much about their first encounter with the enemy but they knew the days ahead would see more killing.

First light saw them on the banks of a raging river. The overnight rain had ceased and the day looked promising. But they were bogged down by the soggy conditions.

Two hours later, Captain Lee called a halt.

'We are not doing too well, are we? Perhaps we should back track and find some higher ground.'

Captain Lee consulted with Charlie before he finalised any plans for each move they made. He had come to rely on Charlie's jungle skills. As they moved through the rain forest, signs of enemy activity were to be seen all around them but by being alert and moving cautiously, they were able to evade the Japs who were hunting them.

However, on the one day he decided to go against Charlie's advice the commandos ran into an ambush. They had lost much time since the dry river bed attack. Captain Lee felt he had to reach their drop zone without further delay. After looking at his map and compass he ordered his troops to press forward towards a heavily-wooded area. There were many tall trees covered with trailing creepers and he surmised those trees would give him additional cover. Gazing at the light, he estimated they had a couple of hours to find a suitable spot to bivouac for the night.

Maake and Ade were sent ahead as trail blazers. Suddenly there was a single crack of a rifle and Maake dropped to the ground. He was dead before he slumped to the wet earth with a bullet through his neck. Then another shot rang out and Ade too fell to the ground. A Japanese sniper had them in his sights.

The commandos hit the ground looking for whatever cover they could find. The slightest movement drew fire and they were pinned down. A quick assessment indicated there was no room for withdrawal, or to try and take out the sniper without losing more of his men. There was also the possibility of more snipers in those creeper-covered trees. They were trapped and the enemy held all the aces. Maake and Ade were taken out like two cherries on an ice cream cone at a seaside fair. But it was too late for recriminations. Haste had already cost them two lives without being able to get off a single shot in defence.

Hugging whatever cover they had and not daring to breathe was getting them nowhere. Charlie realised he had to do something, and do it fast, before the rest of the pack closed in on them. He and Captain Lee had dropped behind a rotting tree stump. Charlie signalled to his leader he would try and circle round to get an angle on the sniper, and when he was ready, Captain Lee was to draw another shot to try and pinpoint the exact location of the sniper's whereabouts. Then he slithered away on his stomach and disappeared into the undergrowth as silently as a cat.

After some tricky manoeuvres, Charlie managed to work his way around carefully, taking care not to snap any dry twigs, or get snagged on the thorny creepers that could give his position away while at the same time getting a fix on his quarry. He knew it would be difficult to spot the sniper until he got very close because of the trailing creepers from the other trees in the vicinity. Suddenly he saw his quarry blending against two thick branches of a huge tree to his left, about 20 feet off the ground and no more than 10 feet way from him with the Jap rifle sticking out from the heavy camouflage he was wearing.

He had done the impossible. Charlie had managed to get himself into a perfect angle to get a shot in. He also knew he had just the one chance to get his man, and if he failed, he was a dead man.

Meanwhile, the main body of the enemy were stealthily converging on his comrades so there was no time to be lost. He gingerly got himself onto his elbows, took careful aim, and got his shot off a split second before the sniper got a fix on Charlie. But Charlie got in there first. His shot hit the target and the body of the sniper crashed to the ground as Captain Lee gave the order to attack.

A fierce gun battle ensued followed by a bayonet charge. Charlie lobbed a grenade in one direction. Then another in a different direction and continued to fire furiously to distract the main force by giving the impression that there were more men with him. His ploy worked, throwing the enemy into disarray. The battle was quickly over and the enemy annihilated.

But the commandos too suffered further losses. They lost Eddie Murphy and John Smith. With nearly a third of their group wiped out, Captain Lee had to use different tactics. If the enemy got too close and they were unable to shake them off, they would leave enough evidence of their whereabouts to draw the enemy in. Once the trap was set, heavily camouflaged snipers in trees would wait to take out as many of the Japs as they could while other commandos would wade in to finish off their pursuers.

These tactics worked well but their own ammunition and explosives, including those that they had availed themselves of from the enemy they killed, was beginning to run low. The need to make haste to their drop zone had become their immediate priority but they had lost Elvis Sampson too. And they were one day behind.

As they approached the drop zone, they stumbled over the bodies of a platoon of British soldiers. From the evidence around them, it became clear that in addition to the supplies they were hoping to pick up, another platoon of commandos had been parachuted in either to link up with them, to reinforce another depleted group, or perhaps to act independently. But the enemy had been waiting for them.

The evidence suggested the platoon had been ambushed the previous day. They also noted that the supplies, so vital for their survival, had been filched by the killers. The Japs had taken the lot.

'I can only guess that Japanese intelligence knew of this drop and were waiting for our men. They did not have a hope in hell by the looks of it,' observed Captain Lee.

'The bastards.' Crawfie looked around him in anger.

'A bloody waste of time,' growled Dougie. 'Those bastards have grabbed our supplies.'

'Not for long if I have a say in this matter,' replied Captain Lee. 'Damned if we let them get away with this. We will go after it. We need those supplies or our mission is doomed. Besides, I think we have a score to settle,' his finger pointed in the direction of the mutilated corpses littered on the ground.

'But, sir,' said Scottie dolefully. 'They have a good head start on us and could be anywhere in this stinking jungle.'

'Maybe. Never throw in the towel even when it appears all is lost. One must strive at all times. Sandhurst drilled this into me. History has shown us time and again battles have been won against impossible odds by doing the unpredictable. A classic example is the charge of the Light Brigade. Attack the enemy when it least expects it. Take them by surprise and take them when they are least prepared. As we have seen in our short engagement here, a platoon can wreak as much havoc as a battalion if you have the element of surprise on your side. If the enemy had any inkling those supplies were for us they would have stuck around to kill us too so let's assume they don't know about us. Find Charlie for me.'

'Yes, sir,' Charlie reported to his commander.

'Charlie, if anybody can find the bastards who did this it has to be you. See if you can pick up their trail. Give it your best shot. We are going after them.'

'I'll do my best, sir.'

'Good man. The rest of you bury your dead compatriots and be quick about it. We have an urgent matter to deal with.'

Their day ended in another bivouac. The group was reduced to six. As was their usual routine, they checked out the area as best they could and gathered enough dry logs for the fire. Logs burned less quickly than brushwood and the glowing embers kept them warm and relatively safe from predators till dawn. They ate their meagre rations and washed that down with steaming hot tea and settled for the night.

Charlie guessed he had been asleep for a couple of hours when he awoke with a sudden start. His instincts told him to stay absolutely still until he raked the ground around him with his eyes for danger. In the ambient light he saw a pair glowing eyes watching the camp site about 20 yards away. It was a big animal but he could not identify what it was. He grabbed a long pole that each man kept handy to deter any animal who got too close and eased the burning tip out of the fire and waved it violently at the animal, which held its ground for a second, then gave out a snarl, turned and loped off into the darkness. Charlie could not tell if it was a tiger or a leopard. The danger had passed.

He settled down to get some sleep but sleep would not come. His mind turned to Penny Webster. It always did in moments of solitude. The other men would talk about the women they had loved and lost, but in the case of Crawfie his conquests always came with descriptions of graphic sexual content. They knew Charlie had a special girlfriend in Ceylon but Charlie declined to talk about her.

As his thoughts raced through his mind, he recalled his first meeting with Penny and the events that followed. His favourite recollection was seeing her naked; her breasts full and round with nipples like tiny rosebuds; her red hair cascading around her shoulders and passion in her green eyes, which she was able to diffuse with a tantalising smile. The perfection of her body always excited him and he felt himself getting aroused. He undid his trousers and turned to his side and used his right hand to ease the tenseness as single men do when there was no woman to comfort them. He wished he could be there in her arms and feel the warmth of her body against him. At such times he regretted his decision to go to England and enlist. He turned over again with a smile on his face and within minutes, the peace he sought came to him with oblivion.

CHAPTER NINE

The marriage of Penny and Philip Webster had run into difficulties recently. Making love was always an important part of their relationship from the first day of their union. Between them they had something intimate and satisfying that they built on during those early years. But in recent months there was a gradual change. The healthy physical intensity that had once been an integral part to their union had slowed down but neither gave it much thought. The lull in making love was bound to happen at some point after so many years.

At first Penny thought it was a temporary phase her husband was going through but as time went on she became aware of the change it was making to their daily lives. Philip was a shy and sensitive man. One of the qualities that drew her to him. She was the initiator during those early years. She made the running, guiding him and teaching on how to take her to the ultimate heights of pleasure. But now, for no apparent reason, Philip had begun to get moody, nervous and edgy, and he had begun to drink more heavily.

Without being too intrusive, Penny tried to find out the root cause for this change but her attempts were brushed aside as he shied away and withdrew deeper into himself. Whatever was worrying him, Penny knew it had nothing to do with finances and business matters. In fact they had more money than they knew what to do with.

Another war in Europe was looming as Hitler flexed his muscles but nobody took him seriously. Then war broke out again for the second time in Europe and Ceylon was sucked in. For a small colony to actually be at war did not make much sense when the unseen enemy was so many thousands of miles away. The war in Europe made no difference to their daily routines. Oh yes, the newspapers and the daily updates on the wireless could not be avoided. The local politicians, mostly those educated in England, were suggesting that Ceylon should be given independence but these men were being influenced by an Indian agitator called Gandhi. Nothing could be more preposterous but the war had made these voices less vociferous. If not unthinkable, then decidedly impractical.

Penny tried to allay any fears her husband may have voiced. Any threat to them would come from the Germans and not from the politicians on their island. The tea industry was the island's biggest revenue earner. Whoever held the reins of power needed the British tea growers and their world markets to sustain it. Their position was safe. But Philip's daily intake of alcohol increased and so did his depression.

Penny's efforts to rekindle some passion in her man failed. Lying next to him night after night, her hugs and caresses, or other feminine ploys failed to arouse any excitement in her husband. She felt rejected. Philip did not want her in the way she wanted him. No amount of cajoling could coax any spark of desire. It was becoming humiliating. She was being deprived of the normal marital relations that had been a major part of their life together. A marriage needed physical love to survive. There was nothing wrong in her expectations. She was a normal healthy woman and she had a right to feel the way she did. In fairness Philip did profess his love for her but his inadequacy drove Penny to distraction.

They had returned to Kandalami after an overnight stay at the Hill Club. While Penny enjoyed herself at the dinner dance in Little England, Philip had got drunk and retired to their room early. What had promised to be a good night out, as it usually did until recently, ended in disappointment.

The next morning, lying next to him, her frustration got the better of her. The time had come when they needed to talk honestly instead of hoping their problems would go away if ignored.

To her surprise Philip agreed. He took her in his arms and held her tightly. He then told her he was impotent. He assured her it had nothing to do with her and she was not to feel in any way responsible for his condition. He said he still loved her and needed her as much as he had ever done. He was sorry but he could not give her the physical affection she craved. Not anymore.

Although Penny had a sneaking suspicion that this could have been the cause, his admission to being impotent came as a complete shock. The finality of this statement said so calmly and without emotion, came as a bombshell to her. She lay there in silence as the gravity of what he had said sank in. But Philip offered no excuses. He had been honest with her. His disinterest in Penny was finally out. He did not know why this had happened but it happened and he was very sorry indeed. He begged her not to leave him.

In a masochistic way they did not have to pretend any more. The constant rejection was beginning to undermine her self-confidence. Philip reminded her of their marriage vows. In sickness and in health, for better for worse, till death do us part. In the privacy of their room they gave in to their pent up emotions as they hugged each other and cried.

From an early age Penny had worked hard to be confident and self-reliant. She knew that if she was to go anywhere in life she would have to be assertive, positive and strong. She resolved to bring these qualities to sustain her. No more pretences. Her marriage had become sterile and she would have to deal with this condition as best she could.

It dawned on her that Philip was the only person she had left in the world to care for her. There was nowhere to escape; no one to run to. Her childhood memories came flooding in. The insecurities she had to grapple with were sobering. No father or mother to love and cherish her. At Kandalami she had a beautiful home, servants at her beck and call and all the material comforts any woman could want, and a man who professed to love her and see to her welfare unlike those lonely years where she was shifted from pillar to post.

But after she and Philip had cleared the air and been honest with each other, it became easier to keep up appearances and socialise as a loving husband and wife. In time, they had turned it into an art form. But away from the limelight, the absence of any passion in Penny's life had begun to put a heavy strain on their daily make-believe existence. She tried hard but occasionally a tension gripped her, which she found increasingly difficult to contain.

Not many moons after their heart to heart chat, Penny felt restless and listless. The weather had changed overnight as she gazed into the swirling mists that covered the mountain range and the valley below. She sensed it was not going to be an ordinary sort of day. As the morning wore on she became increasingly bored. Philip said he had an urgent business trip and had to go to Colombo and did Penny want to accompany him? Penny declined his invitation saying she did not feel too well and the heat of Colombo was the last thing she needed. A few days away from the claustrophobic atmosphere that had engulfed them both could be beneficial not just for herself, but for Philip too. At least for a few days neither of them needed to pretend all was well to the outside world.

Keeping up the sham was getting increasingly hard for her. She was trapped in a loveless marriage and there was no end in sight. She had tried so hard. By God, how she tried. There had to be a way out to keep her sanity. Perhaps she was being unreasonable. But what could she do?

Penny sat down to lunch but could eat nothing. Everything seemed to be closing in on her. Do something, her voice cried out. But what? Anything, but do something.

After half an hour of pushing her food around her plate she got up and went into the garden. The cool clean air felt good and by the time she came in she felt better. Perhaps getting out of the house helped. She had tossed and turned in her bed the previous night unable to sleep. Lack of sleep did not help much either. Suddenly a thought crossed her mind. She decided to drive up to Little England. A change of scenery and some shopping might help. She had decided she would stay overnight as she got ready and packed an overnight case, got into her car and drove away from Kandalami.

There were plenty of goods in the shops despite the war and browsing through the latest fashions was interesting but nothing took her fancy. She returned to the Grand Hotel where she had booked a room. She lay down on the bed and tried to read but her mind kept wandering so she went down to the swimming pool and swam lengths until her body was exhausted. It helped to relax her taut muscles and a short nap made her feel infinitely better. Perhaps that was all she needed. Strenuous exercise.

By late evening Penny had managed to cast aside her depression. Feeling immensely refreshed and back in a buoyant mood, she got ready for dinner in an unhurried manner. She had brought with her the blue, off-the-shoulder dress which highlighted her red hair and tanned skin. It was one of her favourite outfits and she always felt sexy in it. After taking extra care with her make-up, she slipped it on and glanced at herself in the full-length mirror. It brought back memories of happier times. Yes, she had made the right decision to spend the night away from Kandalami. Subconsciously a burden had been lifted. There was a strange sense of relief and freedom as she went down the stairs with a spring in her step.

As she walked through the reception area she noted that the hotel was quieter than usual and she was grateful it was so. The previous day had been Burns Night and she guessed that was probably the reason. Dinner was unhurried and the food tasted good. Perhaps that too may have been because she had hardly eaten anything all day. The night was young and the music emanating from the ballroom beckoned invitingly.

The few people she saw were strangers and that pleased her too. Penny found a table at the corner of the dance floor and settled comfortably into her chair to watch the couples dancing to the music of Cole Porter. A steward came over and took her order for a gin and tonic. By the time her drink was brought to her, the band had progressed to a medley of Victor Sylvester.

The cold shower had invigorated Charlie Digby-Sloan. He felt good as he caught sight of his body in the mirror and flexed his muscles and watched them tighten. He was good looking but not handsome by any stretch of the imagination but he was fit and well with a lean body and the physique of a fit athlete.

He was confident he could make a fair contribution to the important rugby match he was due to play in the following afternoon. Word had got around that the opposition were no pushover. His rivals had been in serious training for several weeks, determined to wrest back the trophy that had eluded them for the past three years. Rumour had it that the new recruits from the lowland plantations were a rough and tough bunch. But Charlie had no fear of the hard tackles to come. He would give as hard as he received. Rugby was a brutal game but brute force alone was not enough to win. Team tactics and skill would see them through.

Dressing casually, Charlie selected a blue and red silk tie to complement his cream shirt and dark suit. Descending the stairs to the right of his room brought him into a small hallway that led to the lobby and from there to the ballroom and the bar.

He was surprised to see Penny Webster sitting on her own at the far end. He assumed she was waiting for her husband to join her. Penny was very much younger than her husband. Many wondered what she found so fascinating in an introverted, older man like Philip. He had not paid much attention but they did look like an odd couple on reflection. Perhaps opposites attract.

He had a few beers and was on his way back to his room when he noticed Penny still seated at her table by herself. Philip had not turned up. It did not surprise him that her husband had given her the slip as he was noted to avoid the bright lights. Charlie was debating whether to say hello when she caught his eye, waved, and beckoned him over. He had noticed Penny had a lithe body and trim figure, and looked very attractive in her swimsuit or tennis outfit but tonight she looked somewhat different to him. Tonight she looked positively sexy. The dress she was wearing hugged her body tightly, enhancing her bosoms and the outline of her hips. The ambiance and the setting and the subdued lighting added to an indefinable aura of hidden mysteries that radiated from a woman feeling sexy.

'Hello, Penny, fancy seeing you here tonight.'

Penny was pleased to see Charlie Digby-Sloan smiling cheerfully.

'You look so lonely sitting here alone. Has Philip abandoned you?'

'Hello, Charlie, where on earth did you spring from?'

'Oh, I was at the bar. I saw you earlier and assumed you were waiting for Philip to join you. I thought it better not to intrude on a cosy evening between the two of you. I hope I'm not intruding now?'

'Absolutely not. Please join me unless of course you have another pressing engagement.' Penny smiled, glad to have someone to talk to.

'So where is your dear husband? You two always gave the impression of being joined together like Siamese twins.'

'Really! Whoever would have thought so,' laughed Penny tossing her hair back and flashing her eyes. 'Philip has abandoned me. Cast me adrift like a ship in turbulent waters. I'm a lost woman now, at the mercy of all the hungry stallions in town.'

Penny could not believe she was uttering these words. She had known Charlie since he was a little boy but looking at him now she saw a mature young man who was attractive in a rugged sort of way. To be truthful she had not really looked at him too closely until now and was quite surprised to see how much he had matured. She was captivated by his boyish smile that came so naturally to him.

Charlie too felt strange, like some adult game was being played. But if that was the way this game was to be played, he was happy to continue.

'Oh come, come, an attractive lady such as you being abandoned. I find it hard to be believe. Not very chivalrous of your husband to leave you at the mercy of men like me.'

'It's true. Philip is not with me. You've had a few beers, I can tell. I wouldn't say my husband was unchivalrous, but this is not his style. Philip is quiet and studious. He prefers his books to the throbbing sounds of primaeval music.'

He knew there was something very different about the Penny Webster, but could not quite figure it out. Perhaps it was the timbre in her voice; or the flirtatious way she spoke to him; or the way she laughed; or the way she crossed and uncrossed her legs. Try as he might he could not work out what made her so different tonight. As she said, it could the beer he had consumed.

'Philip has gone down to Colombo and I was on my own. Everything was so dull and dreary at Kandalami so I thought it would be a good idea that I should have a break too. A spur of the moment thing. Actually, if I was honest with you I craved a bit of excitement. I wished something, anything, would happen to make my existence more bearable. Same old routines that never change. I wished I could make something happen to change all that, but now I need not worry as you have come to my rescue, haven't you Charlie? So very noble and kind. Let's go over to the bar, I need another drink. Besides, I feel so conspicuous sitting here by myself,' Penny said with some urgency in her voice.

'Come on, Charlie.' She took his arm and led him towards the corner of a now almost deserted bar.

'Yes, sir, madam?'

'What will you have, Charlie? Scotch and soda? No, your usual drink is beer but you may prefer something different. A large gin and tonic for me please and whatever this gentleman is having. Put it on my bill.'

'A scotch and soda please.'

'To be honest I could do with some company tonight,' then seeing the surprise on Charlie's face, Penny added quickly, 'Unless, of course you are with someone, or have better things to do?'

'Please may I pay for this?'

'Nonsense, I insist. We live in a liberated age,' said Penny reassuringly placing her hand on his leg. 'I've nursed one drink all evening,' she winked coquettishly as she fibbed.

'Thank you, Penny.'

'No thanks required. Tonight I am in charge of my life. You must think of me being completely out of my mind to behave in this manner but I will let you into a little secret. I've been in the dumps lately and I desperately need cheering up. With Philip away in Colombo I could not possibly stay another moment at Kandalami.'

'As bad as that, eh?'

'Desperately so.' Penny picked up her drink, looked at her glass for a moment, then took a big sip but did not put her glass down.

'I bet I know why you are in town tonight. No, let me guess. Who is the lucky lady? No, don't tell me.'

'I should be so lucky,' laughed Charlie.

'What, no young lady? Of course, it is a secret. I quite understand.'

'No young lady and no secret.'

If Charlie had a girlfriend Penny would have heard about it. There were not many things you could hide in their small community.

'We must do something about it.'

'If you must know I have a rugby match on tomorrow. I did not fancy the long drive from Glencoe. Besides, our coach believes we should conserve our energy for the match. An early night and abstain from—' Charlie did not finish what he was going to say.

'What? You mean sex? Shouldn't make any difference, should it?' Penny raised an eyebrow and looked Charlie straight in the eyes.

'I wouldn't know. I'm neither married nor do I have a girlfriend. The coach said it would keep us mean and raring to go.' Charlie felt his face going crimson with Penny looking at him as she did.

'You can take it from me, Charlie, it makes no difference. I should know.' Penny laughed as she took another big sip of her drink. 'Another round of the same steward.'

Charlie gazed at Penny. He noticed how perfect her teeth were and how her face lit up when she laughed. Penny was attractive all right. Very attractive. She was aware of her own sensuality. The way she flashed her eyes or arched her brows coquettishly, or thrust her breasts forward. She knew how to hold a man's attention.

They watched the steward serve them their drinks and move out of earshot.

'So you spend all your energy playing rugby and having a good time with your mates?'

'Not just rugby. I do lots of other things. I especially like to go into the jungle to track wild animals and to watch the beauty of exotic birds. The jungle is a very demanding environment. Out there survival is the name of the game. Eat or be eaten. Kill or be killed.'

'But shouldn't there be pleasure too? Don't you like girls, Charlie?'

'What are you implying'?

'I am sorry, I did not mean it to sound as it did. Please forgive me. What I meant was have you a special girl? I've seen you with the girls. I just meant, oh, I don't know what I meant. It doesn't matter.'

'If you must know I don't have a special girl. I do like girls very much if you must know. I'm watching you now and I like what I see. What is wrong Penny?'

'I wish I could talk this over with someone, Charlie but there is no one to help me. If you only knew how unhappy I am at the moment. Please don't mention this to anyone but I am seriously thinking of going back to England.'

'Goodness, whatever for?'

'There are reasons, Charlie, but I cannot tell you about them. My life has become very depressing of late. Let's not talk about it. Instead let's have a few more drinks and dance the night away. I know you like to dance because I've watched you on the dance floor.'

'Give me a rugger field to a dance floor any day.'

'You cannot duck out that easily. The night is so pleasant and the music so divine. I feel like one of those hot-blooded gypsies you read about in books. Wild and frivolous, and so passionate. They seem to live without a care in the world. They do as they please and go where their fancy takes them. You know what I mean, don't you?'

'Don't tell me you have gypsy forebears?'

'I don't know, Charlie. I could have. I need to *live*. My only relative was an aunt in Australia, but she has passed away. My father was a mariner and he perished at sea when I was little. I never knew my mother. I never had a family.'

'Sounds as if you had a tough time,' said Charlie sympathetically.

'Yes, and it looks like I'm heading for another. I feel as if I'm in a trap and I want to break free. Come on, Charlie, let's dance before the band packs up for the night.'

'I' m no good at dancing. Besides I've had too much to drink.'

'Nonsense. I want to dance. I want to be wild tonight. There is nothing to it. You put your arms around me and sway to the music. Come on, Charlie. Let me show you.'

Penny got off her stool and walked towards the dance floor giving Charlie no choice but to follow her. Holding Charlie in her arms and swaying to the music made Penny feel warm and wanted again. She was quite excited. The rhythm of the pulsating music did something to her. Charlie was fresh and young and vibrant and easy to please.

They danced a lot that night returning to the bar for a drink from time to time. They were having a good time and it seemed the most natural way to spend a wonderful evening. All Penny's cares seemed to have vanished. Being with a man who was more than 20 years younger than her did not matter. All she felt was being wanted again. Being treated as a woman again. A young man's body pressed against hers brought out all the pent up emotions that had been denied her for so long. She did not want it to stop as her hunger for a man coursed through her body. She hung on to the magic of the moment.

The band had played their last rendition and it was only then that they realised they had been the only couple on the dance floor. The night had turned out to be more enchanting than Penny could have imagined. So wonderful and carefree like times gone by. She was frivolous and passionate and carefree like the times she had so many long years ago and she wanted more.

'You've been so wonderful to me tonight, Charlie. If only you knew how much. You've brought me alive again, excited me, and made me happy again. Please tell me you enjoyed it too? Tell me you did? Wasn't it wonderful for you too?'

'I never enjoyed myself more.'

'I want to thank you for pulling me out of the depths of deep despair and making me feel so good again. How can I thank you, Charlie?'

'No need to.'

'I want to Charlie,' Penny whispered in his ear. 'This night need not end just yet. I don't want it to end. I want it to go on forever. Do you want it to end, Charlie? Do you?'

Charlie said nothing. His evening had been quite extraordinary.

'We can go up to my room and continue our party if you like.'

Charlie could not think straight. He had never known a woman like this could ever exist in any young man's dreams. So passionate. So sexy. So uninhibited. Every fantasy any man could ever dream of.

'Do you think it would be wise? If anyone saw us tongues are sure to wag.'

'I honestly don't give a damn. Come on, Charlie. I need you.'

Charlie saw the imploring look in Penny's eyes and he tried to think of an excuse but there were none forthcoming. His mouth was dry. No words came out. Instead he nodded his head.

Penny took his hand and they went upstairs. Soon they were standing in front of Penny's room. Charlie realised his room adjoined to her own. Penny went in and switched on the lights and then turned towards Charlie.

'Charlie.'

'Yes, Penny?'

'I know you want to run a mile, but please don't go now. Not yet, please.' Penny reached out and took his hand. 'Come with me.'

Charlie knew it was wrong but he went into the room and Penny closed the door silently behind her. She put her

103

arms around him and pulled his head towards her and kissed him on the mouth. He felt her warmth and passion as she pressed herself to him and he kissed her back There was no turning back.

She led him towards the bed kissing him as she undressed him hurriedly and managed to undress herself at the same time.

'Wait a second,' Penny whispered as she unhooked her bra, then took Charlie's hands and placed them on her breasts and stretched her body on the bed. Soon they were making love. It was urgent, it was fierce, and it was over quickly. Charlie could not contain himself. He climaxed quickly. He rolled over and lay panting. Penny turned and lay her head on his chest. They were silent for a while until she spoke first.

'Your first time, wasn't it?' Penny whispered in the darkness. Charlie nodded his head.

'You took me hard.'

'Sorry.'

'Never mind, but it is more pleasurable if you are gentle. There is much to learn about the art of love making. I will show you.'

Penny started kissing him again. First on the mouth. Then she ran her tongue below his ear while her hand moved to his chest. She caressed a nipple and felt it harden. She bent down and kissed it running her tongue around it before biting it gently. He felt her hand slide lower and soon she was caressing the muscles on his thighs, and slipping her fingers between his legs and upwards until she brushed his manhood. It was erect. She caressed it for a moment, then straddled him and made love to him while he watched her gently rocking herself up and down with her knees tightly pressed against the side of his body. Feeling her body move as she moaned with pleasure, pausing at times to prolong and savour the fires of her desires. So uninhibited, so intimate, so natural. Nothing else mattered other than the rising crescendo they both felt within each other. Charlie had never experienced any sensation as intense as this in his life before.

'Oh Charlie, you gorgeous creature. Love me. Yes, yes, don't stop now. Ah, ah,' she gasped as she bent down and buried her head in his neck kissing and biting him gently as she did so. Charlie felt the pain of her fingernails as they dug into his flesh and the frenzy of her orgasm and he climaxed too, soon after.

Lying in each other's arms exhausted, yet completely satisfied, no words were needed as they held each other. Penny had taught him so much that unforgettable night. The events of the night went through his mind as he lay there with his eyes wide open wondering how it all began.

Penny had hugged him even closer during the last dance. He could feel her breasts pressed against him, and their legs and groins rubbing as they swayed slowly to the music. The subtle fragrance of her body intoxicated his senses. She was so feminine and unlike any of the girls he had danced with before. Penny may have been older but she instinctively knew how to excite him as she moved her body against him and thrilled herself on the effect she had on him.

Since reaching puberty Charlie had been intrigued by women. Being a healthy man, his mind was always preoccupied by the way they looked. He was curious about the mysteries that made them so exciting and the warm feelings of arousal his imaginations generated within his loins. His friends were always talking about sex and what they got up to when they were with their girlfriends.

Charlie had never behaved with any girl the way he had with Penny. His attempts and fumbles with the opposite sex never seemed to progress further than a few kisses and caresses. If he was lucky he managed the odd grope. He was 18 years old and had never made love to a woman before Penny. He was intoxicated but nervous at the prospect of what might happen if things progressed further.

This night had changed all his preconceptions on women. The last few hours were magical and unreal. It did not happen. It could not happen. But it did. Such pleasure and such an incredible ending to the night.

At celebrations after each rugby match Charlie had his fair share of booze but it was not the alcohol that made him hot and sweaty. The roar of the spectators from the touchline pumped adrenaline through his body. Physical contact was addictive. So was the excitement. But nothing had ever been like the excitement he experienced in the arms of Penny Webster.

After the third time they had made love, he had fallen asleep. When he awoke, Penny was partially lying on him. His arm was trapped and as he moved it to rid the numbness, Penny woke too. She rolled on her side and massaged the arm with the pins and needles and then put her arms around him and snuggled into him.

'You are a sweet, darling man, and you have made a new woman of me,' Penny whispered in his ear. 'Thank you for being so good to me.'

'It is I who should be thanking you.'

'No, no. You will never know how much this has meant to me.'

'Do you think I should go back to my room now?'

Penny nodded in agreement. 'I don't want you to go but I guess you must. The dawn will be here soon enough and if you don't get any sleep you will be too tired to play in your game. What would your coach say if he saw you now?' Penny could not resist a girlish giggle.

'He won't know unless you tell him. Will you be at the match? Kick-off is at 2:30.'

'I'd love to but I had better not. Perhaps another time.'

'Can I see you again?'

'Do you really want to, Charlie?'

'You know I do.'

'Really?'

'Yes, as often as possible.'

'I don't know, Charlie. You are so beautiful, I could easily have you for breakfast, lunch and dinner. I feel so wonderful and it was you who made it possible. But this is a dangerous game we played. The consequences barely need thinking about.'

'I don't care, Penny.'

'But I do care, Charlie. I don't want you to get hurt.'

'I am a big man now.'

'We will see. Perhaps next Saturday. No, perhaps some time in the course of the week. Yes, I will come shopping next week. I will make an excuse. Meet me in the lobby, early afternoon. I cannot stay the night. If you don't see me it is because I could not get away and not because I don't want to see you. Remember, we have to be very, very careful, Charlie, or we will wreck things not only for ourselves but for a lot of people that we care very much for.'

'I will be waiting.'

'All right, go now.'

Charlie got out of bed and put some clothes on. The rest he slung over his shoulders.

'Before you go, come here.'

They kissed again. Charlie saw Penny's naked breasts. The sight aroused Charlie and he wanted to caress them but Penny giggled again and pushed him away.

'You've got an important match to win, remember? Be good.'

'I'm always good.'

CHAPTER TEN

From an early age Brett Carter came to realise that his family was rather different to those of his school mates. They did not do the usual things that other families did. Like going out on picnics or walks in the country or to the local teashop for scones and cakes. On rare occasions he was allowed to go to the cinema on his own. They had never been to the seaside like Robert Lee, the only boy who came to his defence when other boys ganged up on him.

His father was seldom at home. It was obvious to him, his mother, and sisters that his father actually *preferred* the army to normal family life and would only come home when it was absolutely essential for him to do so. His mother adapted to the long absences and would valiantly try and cope with the lack of her husband's companionship in her own particular way. To Mavis, her husband would fulfil his manly duties in a perfunctory manner like a chore that had to be done. No different to any other routine the army had drilled into him, only this was a routine imposed by his wife.

When Mavis married her dashing army officer, she thought she had gained the passionate embraces of a loving man who would bring gratification and fulfilment to the needs of a passionate woman. Getting satisfaction that was uplifting to the mind and soul and changed the act of procreation into a form of beauty. But this was not to be.

As for the children he sired, it was his wife's responsibility and something she had to deal with. Bringing up children was woman's work, and when they were at school it was the responsibility of the teachers. Major Harold Carter was the breadwinner and in this role he would provide for his family as best he could. There was never any doubt in his mind his responsibilities ended there.

The Carter family could always sense an undercurrent of tension in the home when his father was around. However, to the neighbours everything appeared normal and middle class and very suburban. Not like the other families that lived in their tree-lined avenue. To them, it appeared that the army made too many demands on Major Carter, much to the detriment of his wife and young family. But that was his job. Some people had to sacrifice their lives for the defence of the Realm. It was called dedication to duty. And she was a brave woman coping with her children on her own. Much to be admired. A shining example to all.

When Major Carter returned to his all-too-important duties with the army, the Carter family ditched the tension they were under like the removal of a heavy army greatcoat. A huge weight seemed to be lifted and life got back to normal. Each would return to their normal activities and things would go on as before until he came back. Brett's mother would perk up and be more cheerful, and his sisters would not spend so much time in their bedrooms but would join in the fun and laughter, knowing too well that the disapproving looks of a martinet on their every move was no longer there. They could all relax.

One of the things Brett and his sisters enjoyed most when his father was not around was bath time. He and his sisters would jump in and have great fun with their wooden ships or rubber frogs or plastic ducks. Mavis would let her children have this pleasurable time before bedtime. She would be downstairs tidying up their things and return to make sure her children were tucked up in their warm beds and give each a hug and a kiss. When she had seen that her children had settled down it was her turn for the bathroom before retiring herself.

On warm summer evenings she would be naked when she came out of the bathroom. Nudity never bothered her, unlike her husband who would order his wife to get some clothes on in case the children saw her. At such times Mavis would remind him that God had created her the way she is. She was not ashamed of her body, or the way she looked, and did not feel there was a need to cover up in the privacy of her own home. In fact she was proud of her figure despite having had three children. She *knew* she was still attractive to men. She could see the way the men looked at her when she went shopping. Mavis did not want her children to grow up like her husband. She may not have encouraged her children to walk about the house undressed, but she made it clear to them that there was nothing to be ashamed of, and there was nothing wrong in being naked in the confines of their rooms if they felt the need to dispense with their bedclothes on hot summer nights.

But one bath time was different and it was to stick in Brett's mind. On that particular night they had started their usual games with their toys when something unusual happened. His submarine had disappeared between one of his sister's legs which he retrieved and was lining up to his destroyer when his elder sister pointed at him and started laughing. She found it so amusing she brought it to the attention of her sister.

'Marion, look at Brett,' said Maud giggling and pointing to her brother. 'How did he do that? Look at that standing up so straight.'

Brett had got aroused in the warm water and his penis was erect. 'I don't know, it just happened. Surely you should know by now boys and girls are different.'

'I know boys and girls are different, silly. Boys don't play with dolls,' replied Marion disinterestedly, squirting Brett in the eye with water from her rubber frog.

'It has nothing to do with dolls, Marion,' shouted Maud. 'Girls and boys are different for other reasons but I have never seen Brett like that before. So big and stiff. How did you make it happen?'

'I don't know. It just happens. Perhaps you should ask Mother. Mother knows all the answers and you can ask her. I expect Father knows too but we dare not ask him. You know what he's like. Now watch my sub blow that silly duck out of the water.'

It was customary for Mavis to pop her head in when she thought it was time to coax her children out of the bath. She did not want them catching their death from cold. She also had to tidy up after them.

Maud was still intrigued with Brett's display and asked her mother to explain this to her. This surprised Mavis somewhat but she realised that her daughters were much older than Brett and were nearing puberty. She told them to get ready for bed and come down to the kitchen.

Explaining the differences between boys and girls was not a difficult subject for her to deal with, unlike many mothers she knew. It was all perfectly natural and the children had brought up the subject. It was a good time as any to tell her children the facts of life. She made a mental note to try and make it as simple as she could.

When the children came down there were hot mugs of cocoa waiting for them. She commenced with the reproduction of plants and went on swiftly to animals. She explained that living creatures had to procreate or the species would become extinct. The act of procreation between men and women too followed that of animals but with courtship and social customs. The act of sex could be pleasurable though not necessarily to all, and making babies was not something to be taken lightly.

The children did not understand most of what Mavis had told them but she thought it was adequate for the moment. After the children had gone up to their rooms she made herself another mug of cocoa. She had to find out the facts of life from the servants they employed. She knew her parents would never discuss such an embarrassing subject.

As it turned out, her own sexual experiences were totally different to the bits and pieces of information she was able to glean from them in their kitchen when she became an adult. If only she had known more she probably would not have looked forward to marriage as much as she did. Still, it could have been a lot worse. She had a nice home and three adorable children but she could get no sexual gratification from the man she married.

The sudden death of Major Harold Carter did not seem to have much of an impact on the Carter family except that their finances had been depleted drastically. Her husband's pension would not pay all their bills as their expenses were at the moment. It was a big worry for Mavis. But the situation resolved itself when a wealthy widower claiming to be a distant relative of Harold Carter introduced himself to her.

Brett continued at his school but was never going to keep the family traditions of illustrious army service. He never got to go to Sandhurst. His adult life was blighted by his uncontrollable penchant for under-age girls. It cost him his life when he was murdered by a distraught father.

Robert Lee, who was Brett Carter's defender against bullying, did go to Sandhurst. He fought in a guerrilla action in Burma and was Charlie Digby-Sloan's commanding officer. Captain Robert Lee sacrificed his life to save Charlie after he and Charlie were captured and tortured by the Japanese. He died as a hero as he fought so courageously for his King and the Realm.

CHAPTER ELEVEN

The atmosphere at Kandalami was charged with emotion with Philip at pains to avoid all contact with his wife. Penny was driven to distraction too. Each studiously avoided the other or pretended the other did not exist if they happened to be in the same room. Philip hurt so much that he did not want to be anywhere near his wife. When he was, all he could see was her in the arms of Charlie Digby-Sloan making passionate love. *In flagrante delicto.* She had humiliated her husband in a way that he found hard to comprehend. Now it was up to Penny to find a way in which she resolved this impasse.

She had to bide her time and the opportunity came on the third day after the embarrassing incident. She had had time to appraise her situation. She had no regrets giving into her need for Charlie but she regretted getting found out the way she did. The damage had been done and now it was up to her to try and put things right. To try and salvage something out of the mess she had got herself into.

The meal that night was a strange affair with neither of them eating much but they kept up appearances for the servant's sake. The servants too had noticed that all was not well with the master and the mistress of the house.

She waited until the servants had cleared the dining table and gone to their quarters. She watched Philip pour himself a generous amount of brandy, pick up his book and sink into his favourite chair on the verandah. She pulled up a chair and sat close to her husband but Philip did not get up and walk away as he had done the previous night. Sitting on the verandah was an old routine they had followed for much of their married life. Sometimes talking, sometimes listening to music, sometimes reading or just gazing at the star-spangled sky and listening to the sounds of the night before retiring to bed.

But now there was a need to clear the air and Penny decided she would take the initiative. They could not go on like they had since returning from Little England. She noticed the open book in his hands and saw that Philip had not read a single word.

'Philip, we must do something. Shout at me. Rave and rant. Slap me if it would make you feel better. Do whatever it takes to get this business out of your system.'

Philip pretended not to hear his wife.

'Philip, are you listening? We have to talk, please. We cannot go on like this. What I did was wrong. Very wrong. But I make no excuses. What I have to say will be hard for you to understand. I have never set myself as a paragon of virtue. I have weaknesses like any other person. We are all fallible. I am a healthy woman with needs that you were once so admirably capable of satisfying. I was driven to breaking point. My compulsion got the better of me. I succumbed at a very low point in my life. I cannot change what drives me on or the way I was created. I do not regret what I have done and I certainly do not feel dirty. The act of sex is, and always will be, a driving force within me. You knew that after we were married.'

'I don't think there is anything to discuss, is there?'

'Yes, there is, Philip.'

Philip put his book down on the table and turned to look at his wife. 'Nothing you say will make me feel better. How could you, Penny?' Philip uttered the words with contempt in his voice. 'Picking on little boys now, are we?'

'Charlie is not a boy, he is a man.'

'Why in heavens name, woman? You have everything you need here. I have never stinted you anything.'

'You know why,' Penny's voice was but whisper.

'Are you blaming me for your predicament, is that it? Kick a man when he is down. Rub his nose in the dirt. Humiliate and hurt me. Take my self-respect away. Why don't you take my gun and put a bullet in my brain. That would be infinitely better. Why don't you do just that?'

'You are being silly now. I want us to have a rational conversation. I am not proud of myself but I make no excuses, Philip.'

'How many are there? Whoring yourself to the first person that comes along. You are worse than a slut.'

'I deserve everything you have to dish out but if you must know, Charlie is the only other man I have made love to since we got married. I never looked at another man until—you know. Charlie and I met by accident. It happened. A one-off, or so it was meant to be but—' Penny's voice trailed off again. There was silence except for the night sounds of the tropics that seemed louder than usual in the stillness around them.

'I am your husband for God's sake. Does that not mean anything to you? Do the sanctity of marriage vows mean nothing to you?'

'All of it does, Philip. I am your wife. You brush things aside and hope they will go away but some things don't. You've seen me humiliate myself in front of you night after night but you did nothing about it. Perhaps you derive your pleasure now by seeing me grovel. Well, I am grovelling now.'

'You should know me better by now.'

'We are all created differently. We all have different needs and we survive or fall by these needs. Take these away and what is left? Without the qualities and aspirations that go to make our lives worthwhile, we merely exist. Life is too short for that, at least, it is for me. Some of my needs cannot be pushed aside. There is more to marriage than

115

material things. You know what I'm talking about. Our marriage is no longer normal. I am alive, Philip. My body and my mind need certain stimuli to uplift me. To satisfy my needs. Is it wrong or sinful to deny this? But I am a sinner and I will always be a sinner.'

'And I am a freak.'

'You are not a freak. You have a disability. Love can be spiritual. Love can be physical. I still love you, Philip. My need for Charlie comes from a physical need to release the demons in my body and my mind.'

'You love me? You have a strange way of showing it.'

'We can have companionship, Philip. You are a sensitive person, and if anyone can understand what I'm talking about it has to be you. It is possible to love *two* men at the same time just as it is possible for a man to love two women. In certain social structures men have several wives or concubines while the woman in their lives has to settle for one man. It works for them. I am sure it can work for us.'

'And suppose this is not within my capabilities to comprehend?'

'Then we must talk about it, find a way forward. We have to try and resolve this dilemma if we are to continue staying together. I suppose, in a way, I am relieved you have found me out. Oh yes, I saw the anger and hurt in your eyes, and I do feel an awful compassion for you. I may have even contrived for you to find me out. I did feel bad skulking around while my needs were satisfied. You think I'm a hard-hearted bitch and a slut but you are free to think what you like. Whatever the future holds in store for us, please remember I still love you, Philip.'

'We had a good life together. Why has it all gone wrong now?'

'I don't know the answer to that one. When I married you my sole intention was to be a good wife and a mother and make you as happy as any wife can. We were not blessed by children but that could be down to me. I am not too disappointed in not being blessed with children. I had you and that was all that mattered.'

'Is this supposed to make me feel good?'

'I know nothing will but if we can talk about this we may be able to see each other's points of view. It is important to me for you to know how I feel about you. Please hear me out. After that do whatever you feel you must do.'

'Go on, I am listening.'

'Don't blame Charlie for this mess. As I said, he was there for me when I was at my weakest moment. We are adult and we are civilised, and if we face up to the facts we can cope with this. It won't be easy for either of us nor will it be to our liking or tastes, but if we can compromise we can stay together. Settle for companionship, and perhaps, a new kind of friendship if our love for each other dies.'

'And if that is not possible?'

'You do nothing, Philip. You are perfectly within your rights to kick me out. Perhaps, it would be in everybody's interest if I was to leave Ceylon and try and make another start in England. Would that be preferable to you?'

'I don't really know. All I can see is the most precious person in my life has been taken away from me. Like a thief has crept into my home and robbed me of my most precious possession. My life is with you, Penny. Without you my life won't be worth living. Without you all I can see is despair, desolation and a loneliness that is so unbearable I don't think I could go on living.'

'I did not wish to cause you so much pain.'

'I would have preferred not to have known.'

'It is too late now. I will make arrangements to leave in the morning.'

Again a heavy silence followed. Words were difficult to come by. Each knew of the consequences whatever course they took. For each, the daunting prospect of what lay ahead was what neither wanted. With Philip, she had all the securities she had ever wanted. Were the Gods about to punish her again? Was she going to lose the only home she has ever had?

Penny rose from her chair as she prepared to go inside. On impulse she bent down and kissed Philip on his head.

'Thank you for the wonderful years you have given me. I will always treasure the memories.'

'Don't be silly, Penny. Wait. Please don't go just yet.' Philip got out of his chair and put his arms around his wife. 'Sit with me a bit longer.'

Penny looked at her husband hesitatingly, then sank back into her chair. They sat in silence for a long time.

'You were right when you said we had to talk. I have been thinking. You don't have to go away, Penny.'

'What? I don't understand.'

'I said you don't have to leave. Your place is here at Kandalami. Yes, you can stay with me.'

'How can I? I cannot make any promises that may be broken. I have already broken my marriage vows. There is too much temptation here. Charlie is still here.'

'I know and I am asking you to stay. I cannot bear the thought of you not being here. I need you. Nothing else matters to me. I will not survive without you. Can't you see that?'

'And what if I see Charlie again? I know I will because of my needs. I need Charlie.'

'We agreed compromises had to be made. I have accepted the fact that I cannot give you what you want. So be it. Be discreet and please do not bring him here.'

'Why are you doing this for me? You know you do not have to.' Penny went to her husband and knelt at his feet and buried her head in his lap and she wept uncontrollably.
'I don't want to leave you. I don't want to leave the only home I have ever known. When I told Aunt Agatha all those years ago that you were a kind and generous man, my instincts were right. In your own way you are a bigger man than all of them put together.'

They clung to each other for a long time.

'I have done a lot of thinking since we got back from Little England—' Philip broke off as if he was seeking the right words. 'I guess I drove you into this situation because of my own inadequacies. I had hoped you would cope. My trip to Colombo was to see a specialist. He suggested cold showers and less booze. He also suggested I followed a course of therapy. I haven't got the time to go to Colombo every week for this treatment, whatever that might be. Besides, I don't believe in this mumbo jumbo. I have come to accept my disability and live with it.'

'What if I was cold and frigid? You would probably have done the same. There is infidelity all around us. He who is without sin should cast the first stone. It is wrong for anyone to take the moral high ground? None of us is perfect. None of us is as virtuous as we pretend. But I may not have forgiven you if I caught you in the arms of another woman.'

'I can assure I have no intention of having an illicit sexual encounter even if I was up to it so to speak.' Philip's feeble attempt at humour took away some of the emotional stress they were both under.

Later that night in bed, Philip hugged his wife and she hugged him. Each had reasons of their own for the tears they shed.

A few weeks later.

'I was startled and shocked when Philip burst in on us.'

Charlie and Penny had just made love and were lying in each other's arms.

'I have sorted everything out.'

'What? I don't understand.'

'We were civil, we are adult and we sorted out my problem eventually. Philip is a good man and he loves me. Of course he was humiliated and hurt. Wouldn't you have been if your wife was with another man? He saw that none of us is perfect. We all have failings.'

Charlie shook his head in disbelief. He was expecting something terrible. 'So everything is fine?'

'Everything is not fine Charlie but Philip and I have come to an understanding.'

'What understanding? What does this mean?'

'Listen, nobody knows about us except Philip. We can see each other but we have to be very, very discreet. Please don't ask me to go into details.'

'Bloody hell. If you were my wife and I caught you with another man I would have broken your neck.'

'I am not your wife, Charlie.' Penny's voice was soft but there was no mistaking her meaning.

Their new relationship was mutually accepted. Life at Kandalami went on as serenely as before.

Time had stood still for a short time but the monsoon weather had stopped as quickly as it had started. The depleted team knew in their hearts their task ahead was insurmountable. They also knew that they would not survive for long. They would be either killed or captured but their part in this war was nearing the end.

Some days later the men stumbled on a well-made road. Captain Lee ordered his men to fall back and take up positions to observe the traffic and strength of the enemy that used it. His map and compass indicated that they were about 200 miles south of Rangoon which was the next main Japanese objective if they were to capture India.

Before long they witnessed many trucks of heavily-armed Japanese and armoured vehicles speed through, heading in the same direction as the commandos. Some were laden with supplies while others carried personnel. A reconnaissance later showed a large construction of sorts was underway close to a big river, which was heavily guarded by a garrison on both banks.

Captain Lee decided it was too dangerous to proceed further. To mount any attack would be suicidal. They fell back. He reckoned that this was a job for the main force of the allies to deal with. But he could move his small force further south and mount a guerrilla action to disrupt some of the vital supplies getting through.

The watchers also saw Japanese patrols rounding up and summarily executing any peasants who got too close to this strategic landmark.

'Men, we have observed all the activity that has been going on in this sector. We have been breaking our backs carrying all these explosives and don't you think the time has come for us to unload this burden? Our targets will be the road we have seen, any communication lines we come across and fuel dumps we find. We cannot stop them from whatever mischief they are up to but we can do our best to slow them down. Hit them hard and retreat into the jungle. Oh yes, they will come after us but if we plan our operations with due care and attention, we could draw the enemy into an ambush and take a few more out. Timing and venue will be of the utmost importance and we strike when it suits us. Any comments?'

'Let's have some action, sir. It's better than being eaten alive by the unseen enemy buzzing round our ears.'

'It is the only way now. We're outnumbered but we have come this far not to sit on our hands.'

'Yeah man, we're up to our necks in deep shit so let's go down fighting. Take as many of those bastards as we can.'

Captain Lee listened in silence while his men voiced their opinions. His options were limited but his orders were specific.

'Thank you gentlemen for all your suggestions. We will deal with each situation as it arises. It is a case of taking our chances but I want no heroics. Let's get back to where we saw those convoys first. The terrain is rough with plenty of cover. We can hit them there and melt into the undergrowth. For the immediate future we concentrate on the trucks carrying the materials. Those are slower and bigger and an easier target to destroy. It will also have a bigger impact on their progress. Right let's get to it. Any comments?'

There were none.

The laying of mines, setting detonators and the concealment of them was much easier than first anticipated due to the rain-sodden earth. The commandos never used the same stretch of road twice. Soon they honed the art of picking the right trucks and timing the detonators until all their explosives were exhausted. The enemy increased their patrols but the thick jungle gave the commandos the cover they needed to hit them hard and withdraw. Their enemy gave chase but all to no avail. If the conditions and the terrain was suitable, they were even able to turn the tables on their pursuers and ambush them. Their short campaign was a great success but their explosives had run out and their ammunition running low. The weapons they took from the dead were not always as effective and often unreliable.

After one such raid to avoid the Japanese patrols that had stepped up their search, they chanced upon a meadow. In the distance was a cluster of peasant huts and to the left of it a rice paddy. As they edged forward, they saw a single man ploughing the paddy field with two water buffaloes. Near one of the huts were a few women and children sheltering from the sun under a tree. A few chickens scratched in the dirt and a pig wallowed in the mud at the edge of the field being ploughed. The setting was rural and peaceful.

'On a day like this it feels good to be alive, wouldn't you say, Crawfie?'

'Struth matie, you wouldn't say there was a war on. George, look at that scene of tranquillity over there.'

'And those chickens pecking way. I ain't tasted chicken for so long I've forgotten what it tastes like,' George laughed.' I would give an arm and a leg to get my hands on one of those chickens.'

'Yeah man, me and all,' Brandon rubbed his hands in glee.

'Quiet,' hissed Charlie holding up a hand in warning.

'What's up, Charlie?'

'Take another look, sir. Something smells. See that man ploughing the field? He keeps looking towards those huts anxiously from time to time. See those women and children? The women appear to be old and the children very young. Why are they sitting around doing nothing? From the number of huts there and the number of women and children you would think there would be more than one man. Also, there should be younger women who produced those children. To me it looks very suspicious. I will bet a month's pay there are Japs lurking about in there.'

'Blimey matie, what's the matter with you? Cracking up or something. Do me a favour, will you. I smell a hot meal of chicken and boiled rice waiting for us. Perhaps, a few fresh vegetables too.'

Crawfie looked peeved.

'Crawfie, you go in there and you will get more than a hot meal. More likely you will end up with a gut full of hot bullets. Look at it. The whole scene stinks.'

'Drop back men, Charlie could be right. We have been a pain in their backsides for the past few months and those cunning bastards will try any trick to get us. You underestimate them at your peril. Have you learned nothing from this campaign? If there are Nips in there we will soon know for sure. If there are more peasants they are probably being held in one of those huts. Let's circle round and take another look from a different angle. If the Nips are waiting for us they must have worked out we were heading in this direction.'

'Oh man, seeing those chickens has made my tummy rumble,' Freddie muttered.

'Stop whinging, I'm as hungry as you are.' Crawfie dropped to his knees looking around sharply.

The men skirted the paddy field while taking great care not to be seen by the lone ploughman working it. Keeping the field between them and the huts gave them cover and a better chance of escape. The men knew there would be sentries posted and a sniper in a nearby tree. A lesson they had learned the hard way that now seemed such a long time ago. But there were no tall trees around the route Captain Lee had taken.

As they approached cautiously, sure enough, the Japanese were crouched behind some boulders close to one of the huts at the far end.

'We can take them, sir. It will be a piece of cake,' Dougal whispered to his commander.

'Not this time, Dougie. I have to think of those peasants. If we did there will be reprisals. We are here to take on the enemy but we don't want any innocent people killed if we can help it. We will have ample time for that later. Back off.'

'Aw, there goes my chicken meal,' grumbled Crawfie.

Captain Lee chose to ignore Crawfie's remark. The men had devised many ruses to distract their foe while their explosives lasted, but now this form of operation had come to an end. Instead they had resorted to luring the Japanese patrols searching for them in different ways. A favourite ploy was to build a small camp fire with a dead animal roasting on a spit. The spot would be carefully chosen. It would be late evening, just before dusk, and there would be a light breeze wafting the smoke through the trees. They would take up strategically-deployed positions and wait to spring their trap. Only the stupid British would light a fire with them about. The Japanese would be drawn into what they thought was an easy target only to find themselves surrounded, but it took meticulous planning.

Usually, Charlie and Crawfie would be perched high in a tree giving signals as to the whereabouts of their quarry and this trick never failed. But there was one time when Charlie detected a larger than normal force trying to encircle them and they'd had to abort their ambush and get away in the nick of time in the gathering gloom. They only just escaped. This time it was much too close for comfort.

Perhaps the men had become too complacent because of the success of these raids. Or it could have been because of the unrelenting heat and humidity and their constant struggle with flies, mosquitoes, leeches, scorpions, ants and other insects that made their daily lives unbearable.

Or perhaps they were extremely exhausted and battle weary. Their campaign had been hard and long, and now they were low on ammunition, and whatever scraps of food they had was almost depleted. Or it could have been their luck had finally petered out. The enemy had their drop zones covered and the prospect of getting any supplies was more or less non-existent.

Their last encounter resulted in a running battle in which Freddie, Scottie, George and Brandon were lost. Now left with just four of the original group, their odds of survival had diminished and their only hope was to elude the enemy until allied troops arrived, or try and join up with similar groups if there were any in their part of Burma. They had heard and seen aircraft high in the sky but they had not seen any evidence of British commandos on the ground.

A few days later the remaining four ran into an ambush. They had been making slow progress by a fast-flowing river in search of fruit or the possibility of catching fish. The men had not eaten for the last two days when they finished their last dry biscuit. They needed sustenance if they were to evade those pursuing them.

Suddenly there was a burst of gunfire and Charlie saw Dougal take a direct hit and topple into the river. The other three dived into the rain-swollen river and made their escape by scrambling onto the opposite bank further down, but in the process they had lost whatever kit they had and all their weapons. Now they had nothing to fight the Japanese with except their bare fists.

Having regrouped, they knew their situation was extremely bad. Each knew that time had run out for them although no one put it into words. Their battle with the enemy was approaching its conclusion. The end was not far.

Later that night Captain Lee congratulated his two remaining men. 'We can get much satisfaction from our contribution to this war. We acquitted ourselves with much merit,' Captain Lee spoke with pride in his voice. 'We've given our finest, and done our best, but we cannot fight the enemy without guns and ammunition. I know that we slowed down the enemy with immense courage and tenacity against insurmountable odds. We lost brave comrades who fought bravely for King and country. You all deserve the highest medal for gallantry and supreme courage. I have been extremely proud and privileged to be associated with you. Your courage and fortitude in the face of a formidable enemy is much admired. I need say no more.' Captain Lee smiled, went to each of his two comrades and shook them by the hand.

'Our final task is to try and get back to our own lines wherever that might be. Our other option is to get to the coast and hope to be picked up by one of our boats. Get as much rest as you can. We leave first thing in the morning. Thank you.'

Even in the face of defeat Captain Robert Lee held himself erect. The determination they saw on his face was not lost on Crawfie and Charlie.

The next morning the three men headed in a westerly direction. With no map or compass, they used the sun as a directional aide or followed the course of rivers. They hoped to scrounge food from friendly villagers and perhaps hitch lifts in their precarious little boats. But they had hardly made any progress when they were surrounded by a Japanese patrol and surrendered expecting a quick bullet to the head. Instead they received a severe beating.

When they regained consciousness, they found themselves bouncing about in the back of an army personnel carrier. Charlie guessed they were being driven to the nearest camp for interrogation. To him, a bullet to the head would have been infinitely preferable. He then lapsed back into merciful unconsciousness.

CHAPTER TWELVE

Over the last three months Penny could sense a subtle change in her young lover. The frantic eagerness of a boy had changed into the assertiveness of a mature man. The lingering kisses and caresses and endearments were still there but she could feel a restlessness in Charlie that had imperceptibly crept in.

They had managed to meet at one of the secluded spots near Glencoe but the last time this happened their love making was quick and when it was over Charlie got off the blanket on the ground and walked towards the edge of the gorge. Penny knew there was something on his mind other than the view below.

'Is something the matter, Charlie?' Penny joined him at the rim and looked into the sheer drop below them.

'Nothing. You were as wonderful as ever.'

'So were you. A penny for your thoughts.'

'Should be a guinea or better still a gold sovereign. You are worth more than a penny to me.'

'So I'm worth something to you, eh?' Penny linked her arm around him. 'Tell me what you are thinking.'

'Oh, this and that. You know there is a war right on our doorstep.'

'I know,' she looked into his eyes. 'What's that got to do with you and me?'

'A lot. Those bloody Japanese have got their eyes on us. They've overrun most of the Pacific islands. They've taken

Singapore, Burma and Thailand. Ceylon will be next. We must do everything we can to stop them. I should do something to stop them. Talking about it while sitting comfortably on our verandahs sipping tea is not going to get us far. Tens of thousands are dying out there. Men, women, and children.'

'Perhaps,' Penny ignored the scorn in Charlie's voice. She knew he was right. 'The British and our allies are doing all they can.'

They looked at the view silently. There was something serious on Charlie's mind by the tone of his voice, but Penny was afraid to probe too deeply. He sounded cold and distant. Perhaps Charlie was tiring of her and looking for a way out. Things had not gone too well recently. Is he trying to end their relationship? No, Charlie needed her as badly as she needed him. They were two of a kind. Maybe their assignations were not ideal but their options were limited.

'Do you still love me, Charlie?'

'Of course I do. You know I do.'

'You've not told me so lately.'

'I love you very much, Penny. I will always love you until the day I die.'

'So what is this problem? I sense you are wrestling with something serious.'

'I am going to enlist and fight for what I believe in. You, me, my family, my country, and my heritage. I am not going to lie down and let the Japanese take what is mine.'

'I thought you were getting tired of me and wanted a way out.'

'You silly goose. I feel compelled to do something for my country. It is my bounded duty. One of the Digby-Sloans must demonstrate their loyalty to their flag. Dad is too old to fight. Rupert? Can you see him with a gun in his hand? Dad will need him with so many of us signing up.'

'Have you told your parents?'

'Not yet. You are the first to know.'

Penny was nonplussed by this startling announcement. She saw that Charlie must have spent much time thinking this through. 'Why don't you think this over a bit longer. Then perhaps, you should seek your parents' views.'

'This is a matter that only I can decide for myself.'

'So anything I might say will not make you change your mind?'

'I am prepared to hear what you have to say but don't you realise how serious a situation we are confronted with?'

'Your head is ruling your heart not your heart ruling your head. Laugh and the whole world laughs with you. Cry and you cry alone.'

Charlie laughed but there was no mirth in it. 'You could have used that cliché at a better time but I assure you a lot of tears will be shed before this war is over.'

'Obviously you have thought this through and anything I say is not going to stop you. If that is the case then you must do what you feel you must do. Remember, wherever you are, I will be with you. When you see that lone star in the sky I'll be looking at it too. Remember that, Charlie. And I will be waiting for you when you come back.'

'I may never come back.'

'I know you will come back to me and I will be waiting for you, Charlie. My Charlie. I will weep for you during my moments of anguish. The memories of your arms around me I will take to bed each night. There will be many dark days and sleepless nights for me. Perhaps for you too. Remember I will be with you during those moments, my love.'

'Will you do me a favour?'

'You've only got to ask. You know I will.'

Charlie hesitated. 'Will you see me off? I don't mean here. From Colombo. Let's spend my last few days in Colombo together where we can really be ourselves away from prying eyes. The warm sea of the Indian Ocean. That beautiful golden sandy beach and the waving green palm trees and you by my side is the memory I wish to take with me until I return to you. That and all the memories we have shared together. Will you do this for me?'

'I will.' Penny nodded her head as her eyes misted over. Nobody mattered at that moment but Charlie.

'Dad, Mum, everybody,' Charlie waited until he had the attention of all in their drawing room. 'I have decided to enlist and fight in this war.'

A deathly hush engulfed the room as they looked at Charlie with disbelief. His mother was the first to break the silence. 'Why do you want to go and do something like that Charlie?' she enquired gently. 'There are so many other ways to help win this war. You don't have to carry a gun and kill people.'

'Your mother is right. Producing tea is important. The production of food and essential supplies are as important as carrying a rifle or making bombs and guns and war planes and destroyers.'

'Someone from this family has to fight for King and country. Fight for what we believe in. Fight to protect what we have. I have come to the conclusion, after much deliberation, I should be the one to do it. I'm not disputing what you say, Dad, but without men to fire the guns we will lose this war. See what the Japanese have done, and are doing, to our compatriots in Hong Kong, Singapore, Thailand, Burma, and all the other islands in the Pacific. I would rather be out there than wait for Japanese to do the same to us. If they invade Ceylon, we can say goodbye to all that we have now. I don't want that to happen to anyone of us. I would rather die fighting than sitting on my hands doing nothing.'

'We have enough men and machinery from all parts of the British Empire to fight this war. The Germans or the Japanese are not going to walk all over us. But if you feel that is what you have to do then you must do it. You have my blessing. To fight and die for your country is an admirable and honourable thing to do. We have been doing this for centuries.' His father looked around the room for support. His mother looked at her husband sadly but nodded her agreement. His two siblings did the same.

Kylie rushed to Charlie and put her arms around her brother. 'You silly old sausage. You have always chased a cause. We will miss you terribly.' There were tears in her eyes.

'Don't be daft you soppy old thing. The Germans won't get me. Neither will the Japanese.'

Charlie smiled with relief.

Rupert too came and put his arm around his brother's shoulder. 'They are not big enough to mix it with the Digby-Sloans,' there was unbridled admiration in his voice.

'Thanks, both of you. Rupert, you are now in charge. Make sure you keep an eye on Dad, Mum and our kid here.'

'Hey, I'm not a kid any more, and I don't need any eyes kept on me, thank you very much,' replied Kylie, pretending to be mortally offended.

As the eldest son, his parents understood why Charlie had to lead the way. It was a matter of honour. But they too saw the determination in their son. Nonetheless his mother was astonished as was his father, brother and sister.

The date for Charlie's departure to England was fast approaching. Posters at the Planters Club announced *carte blanche* that all were welcome to join the Digby-Sloans to wish Charlie *bon* voyage.

'Philip,' Penny spoke to her husband tentatively, 'you are probably aware that Charlie is leaving for England. The Digby-Sloans are having a farewell party for him at the Planters Club. Will you be going?'

'I don't think so. Under the circumstances I don't think my going would be a wise move. Make a plausible excuse for my absence but don't let me stop you.'

'We've been good friends with them for a very long time. It would be a nice gesture if you were there too.'

'I won't be going, Penny.'

'Charlie is their first born. They were quite shaken when he made the announcement. They are putting on brave faces but in their hearts they know Charlie could be killed.'

'Such things are known to happen in wars,' muttered Philip not wanting to be drawn into further discussion. It would put a halt to the current impasse. Philip hated every moment his wife spent with Charlie.

'I suppose you will be glad. It's not only soldiers that die in wars but many innocent civilians too. Let's not feel too safe and snug. The Japanese are closing in on us and we too can be killed at any time.'

'At least he is trying to acquit himself with some honour.' Philip grudgingly acknowledged.

'Would you rather I did not go?' Penny enquired.

'It would be too conspicuous if none of us went. Why prompt unnecessary enquiries. No, this is your scene and I know you will not want to miss this one.'

'There is no need for sarcasm, Philip. These people are our friends. They should not be held responsible for my indiscretions.'

'Of course, we must keep up appearances, shouldn't we?'

'I got your drift, I will go.'

On reflection Penny was glad her husband decided not to attend Charlie's farewell. She could relax and be her normal self without having to look over her shoulder to see what Philip was up to. The strain would make him drink more than usual and that could lead anywhere.

The farewell party for Charlie was lavish. While all their guests were having a good time, the Digby-Sloans put on brave faces. The possibility of their son not returning was never far from their minds. The strained smiles that Clara conjured from time to time masked the anguish she felt. James consoled himself with pride for his eldest boy and he knew he would have done the same if he was a younger man. Charlie appeared to be unconcerned and joined the frivolity and fun that the Planters Club was always able to provide its patrons.

'You said you will meet me in Colombo.' Charlie had managed to single out Penny for a brief moment. 'In four days' time I embark for England. I have some friends to see and other formalities to complete before I leave these shores.'

'Will your family be there to see you off?'

'No. I specifically told them I did not want them there when I sailed. It would have been too upsetting and I did not want there to be a fuss. It is bad enough as it is. I will be going down tomorrow.'

'Where will you be staying?'

'At the Mount Lavinia Hotel. Dad arranged it as a sort of farewell present. If you do make it please stay at another hotel. We have to be careful, remember? If we run into someone we know we can make it look like a coincidence.'

'I will meet you in Colombo. I have sorted it out with Philip so there is nothing to worry on that score.'

The overnight sleeper to Colombo was not her ideal way of travelling and it was the first time she had travelled to the capital by herself. She took a rickshaw from the Fort Railway Station to the Galle Face Hotel and booked into a room facing the ocean.

The three days she spent with Charlie were memorable, cramming as much as was possible in the short time they had left. Sharing uninhibited moments of intimacy, frolicking in the warm waters of the Indian Ocean, strolling hand in hand on the golden sand, or lazing under coconut palms as the breezes cooled their partially naked bodies. It was heavenly while it lasted.

When it was time for Charlie to leave, they hugged and kissed each other tenderly promising to continue from where they left off. To be faithful, to be celibate, and to wait for each other until his return. But Penny's resolution to hold her emotions in check failed as her eyes welled up in tears. She hated the war. She could not comprehend why sane people wanted to kill each other in the name of a good cause. She waited until the steamer sailed out of sight over the horizon as the sun followed in its wake in crimson colours.

From her hotel room, she gazed out to sea knowing her lover was beyond her reach. A lot of tears were shed that night. The next morning she packed her bag and returned to Kandalami.

'Enjoyed your final fling?' Philip enquired by way of a greeting.

Penny was silent. There was nothing to say.

'Has he gone now?'

Penny nodded her head. 'Please, Philip, not now. I'd rather be left alone if you don't mind. We did agree, didn't we?' she looked imploringly at her husband. 'Can we not talk about it?'

'I'm sorry. I was worried something might have happened to you. I want you to know I'm glad you are back.'

'How could you say something like that after the way I have behaved? I'm not very proud of myself so please don't make me feel worse.'

'We all have compulsions. Mine is drink. Care to join me? I've had a few already.'

'No, I want to curl up and die.'

'Nonsense, you've enjoyed every moment of it. Perhaps, you will be more sociable in the morning.'

The next few days were subdued but gradually Penny came to accept that Charlie had gone out of her life. It was his choice and there was no way she could have prevented him from going. She had tried. Her life had changed again. Perhaps it was for the best. Sooner or later their affair would have become public knowledge. She knew the chain reaction that would have caused. It amazed her to think that they were able to keep their secret trysts and had not been discovered for so long. At times she accepted the fact that

that phase of her life was over but the sadness she felt was never far away.

But in the days that followed, she and Philip noticed a different atmosphere at Kandalami. The tension that followed her return from Colombo had gradually disappeared. Charlie was no longer a barrier between them. But soon another shock awaited Penny and Philip. She discovered she was pregnant. She was carrying Charlie's baby. The bouts of nausea each morning soon confirmed this.

The thought of breaking this news to her husband was going to be difficult but he would have to know sooner or later. She decided to pick the right moment to drop this new bombshell. Though the emotional strain had subsided in her husband she noticed that he had sunk deeper into depression.

One evening as they followed their daily ritual of sitting on the verandah after a quiet dinner, Penny thought the time was right.

'Philip, can we talk? There is something you ought to know.' Penny spoke softly.

'Listen, Penny, we agreed not to talk about what you get up to. If you don't mind I'd rather not hear what you have to say.'

'I know, but what I have to tell you is very important.'

'If it is about another man I'd rather you kept that information to yourself.'

'There is no other man.'

'You surprise me.'

'I know. I'm full of surprises but what I have to tell you came as a bigger surprise to me.'

'Well, what is it this time?' Philip looked at his wife cautiously.

'When we were newly married, you remember, we spoke of starting a family. We tried ever so hard but it was never to be.'

Philip had always expressed the wish of having children but none materialised. Now he was impotent so the matter never cropped up again. Perhaps it was his fault. Penny assumed it was she who was infertile.

'We tried but I suppose I'm to blame for that too. All your misfortunes since our marriage appear to be my fault.'

'No, I'm not saying it was your fault. I assumed it was me, and I had given up hope of ever having babies. Honest.'

'So why talk of something that is never going to happen.'

'But it has happened. Philip, I think I'm pregnant.'

To say that Philip was surprised would have been an understatement. He was astonished. He could not believe what he had just been told. It had not sunk in.

'Did you hear what I said?'

'I heard you, Penny. You think you are pregnant. You must be mistaken.'

'At first I thought so too but this is no phantom pregnancy. I have all the positive signs.'

'What do you want me to say?' Philip was still digesting the astonishing news. 'Congratulations?'

'I thought you ought to know, that's all.'

'Crikey. Is that all, woman?' Philip got out of his chair, then sat down again. 'Blimey, whatever next. I need to think.' He laughed nervously, got out of his chair again and helped himself to a stiff drink from the sideboard, came back and slumped into his chair again.

'I have to know where I stand, Philip. Please don't ask me to get rid of my baby. I want it desperately, and I hope to God it is born healthy. In spite of my sins, God has blessed me with the greatest gift of all. The gift of life. A baby I have always wanted and was never able to have until now.'

'Blimey.'

'I wish you'd say something sensible.'

'What can I say? If it is God's will, who am I to go against His wishes.'

Penny looked anxiously at her husband but Philip was still trying to come to terms with this new twist in his life.

'I need to know where I stand. I want this baby and I'm going to keep it.'

'No reason why you shouldn't. You do not trifle with the gift of a new life.'

'Can I stay here or will I have to go way?'

'Who said anything about going away?'

'I can stay here then?'

'Of course you can. You know I will stand by you no matter what.'

'Thank you, Philip.'

'Come to think of it a baby in this house might take our minds off our own worries. Yes, the more I think the better it sounds. It will give us both something to focus on. There is no reason that anyone should know the baby is not mine. This is nobody's business but our own. We will not only keep the baby but we will cherish it and give it the best start in life we can.' Philip got out of his chair and went over to his wife. 'A gift from the Gods, eh? We cannot refuse gifts from the Gods.'

Philip bent down and kissed his wife gently on her cheek. 'Congratulations.'

Penny turned towards her husband and looked at him seriously. She could not detect any trace of scorn in his face.

'Yes, a youngster running around Kandalami will be a new experience. A baby after all these years. I cannot believe it.'

'Thank you, Philip. You have proved yet again you are a bigger man than all of them put together.'

'Yes, dear,' laughed Philip whimsically. 'If you say so, my dear. For better for worse we stay together.'

CHAPTER THIRTEEN

The prison camp comprised of makeshift bamboo and mud huts clustered in rows in a jungle clearing and enclosed with a high perimeter fence of barbed wire patrolled by sentries working in pairs. Each corner of the compound was dominated by a raised platform manned by machine guns. At one end were the guards' quarters and next to those was a better constructed hut with a flagpole flying the Japanese flag.

Before long Charlie got to know it housed the despotic, brutal and blood thirsty camp commandant by the name of Colonel Sugihara. As he familiarised himself with his new surroundings, he noticed several stout posts between the guards' quarters and the camp commandant's hut. He did not have to wait long before he saw what those posts were used for. Torture. Prisoners were tied to these posts by their hands or hung upside down by their ankles. All were beaten and tortured and made to endure the relentless heat for days without food or water depending on the seriousness of their misdemeanour. Many were cut down after death.

Colonel Sugihara controlled his camp with terror and fear not only to his prisoners but also the guards. Over the next two weeks Charlie came to dread the daily routines, which never changed from one day to the next. At daybreak each prisoner would be given a bowl of watery rice, then lined up in the compound for inspection by the camp commandant and then marched out to work on the road or other constructions in the area. Those who were fit and strong were grouped for work. The second group would be taken out, many helped or dragged by their comrades or guards in a different direction into the jungle. These men were never to return to the camp again.

Talking amongst prisoners was strictly forbidden. Anyone breaking this rule would be beaten to the ground or received a rifle butt to the head or was tied to one of the three punishment posts.

After two days of interrogation, Captain Lee and Charlie were returned to the main body of prisoners. Colonel Sugihara accepted their story of being parachuted a few days before their capture. They had been blown off course and had been separated from their unit. This was their previously rehearsed cover story in case of capture which they stuck to however unbearable the torture.

Among the guards it was common knowledge that Colonel Sugihara was a member of the feared *kompetai* (secret service). His power was absolute and the guards treated him like a God. His slightest command brought fear into their eyes. He expected total obedience and any guard slow to carry out his orders did not escape his wrath or his punishment. New prisoners soon became aware of Colonel Sugihara's methods of running his camp. He was an expert in torture; his methods barbaric. Death was a welcome release to those selected for his special attention during his frequent rages. At such times victims were selected at random and tied to the punishment post to await whatever punishment took Colonel Sugihara's fancy. Sometimes even examples of his own guards were made if any dared to question his authority.

Due to the harsh conditions many were driven out of their minds. Others deliberately took the easy way out by rebelling. The earth around the punishment posts was dark in colour with the amount of blood it had absorbed. Crawfie was defiant until his last breath. He took the easy way out. Having suffered the post for two days he knew his chances of survival was slim. He was still alive when the guards cut him down and made to kneel at Colonel Sugihara's feet. His samurai sword came down and the earth ran red with blood. Crawfie died while the rest watched in silence.

The work was hard and brutal and never varied from one day to the next. Captain Lee and Charlie tried to stay close together and would urge each other on with looks or gestures when fatigue got the better of them. But it was apparent right from day one that survival for any length of time under these conditions and near starvation would be short. They were cheap labour and expensive to feed and death was an easy way to eradicate a problem.

The two quickly mastered the art of talking in snatches with their heads in their chests, or from underneath their arm pits when bent over. At night they bolstered their spirits by making plans to escape at the first opportunity that came their way.

Soon they worked out a plan to break out during the next tropical storm. They observed that many of the guards took cover during heavy torrential downpours. The lightning flashes would help them to see where the sentries were and the thunder would cover any noise they made. They were also aware that during such storms the power from the kerosene generator short-circuited the wiring from time to time. Captain Lee and Charlie agreed that if their plan was to succeed, their only way out was from one of the machine gun towers. The rolls of heavy barbed wire stopped at each of the four towers. Both would have to scale the tower unobserved and silence the guard before he had the chance to open fire.

Their whole plan depended on this one strategy. They witnessed other futile attempts fail in a hail of bullets. Once they had taken out the machine gunner it was easy to jump down the outer side and race into the jungle before the lights came back on. The distance the two would have to cross was about 70 to 80 yards. With the machine gun out of action, they would have the vital few seconds to get clear before the guards on the perimeter boundary opened fire.

Charlie had managed to find a thick piece of bamboo which he fashioned into two daggers and concealed them under a layer of earth close to their sleeping area. If they could grab any weapons from the disabled machine gunner that would be a huge bonus. The plan was to head for the river and try and reach the coast travelling by night, disguised as peasants, and survive on whatever food they found in the jungle. Their odds for survival, they reasoned, were better than any they could hope for in the camp.

After what seemed like an eternity, the day for their escape unexpectedly dawned. The morning was bright, stiflingly hot and humid, but by the time they returned to the camp after another day's gruelling work, the dark clouds had started to pack in showing all the signs of a big storm brewing.

The prisoners were unusually restless and irritable as they toiled in the unrelenting heat. Constant interruptions were summarily followed by much brutality. Seeing four of your comrades being clubbed to death only made them more angry. To make matters worse their meal of watery rice was barely cooked and contained many dead insects. As the dark clouds rolled in and the sky blackened, the atmosphere in the camp became tense and electric as the impending storm gathered pace. Everybody sensed that something dramatic was about to happen.

Suddenly, without any warning, one of the prisoners rushed to the barbed wire fence in a futile attempt to escape. The sentries followed their usual routine and cut him down in a hail of bullets. This was followed by hysterical shouting from the rest of the prisoners, which was the catalyst for a dreadful sequence of events to happen.

The ensuing commotion brought an enraged camp commandant from out of his hut. The weather had got to Colonel Sugihara too, whose uniform was soaked in sweat. He was unsteady on his feet from the *sake* (rice wine) he had drunk. Also, he was wearing his now familiar *hackimaki* (white silk headband) worn by the samurai, which became the signal to those who had been in the camp long enough to know the commandant had found his excuse to reinforce his authority. He strode out with fury blazing from his eyes. He ordered his guards to line up the prisoners, then marched up and down the line raving and ranting, sometimes in broken English, as he worked himself into an hysteria.

'So you want trouble? I will give you trouble. The penalty for talking is a beating. The penalty for trying to escape is death, not only for those trying to escape but also the payment of a forfeit for the foolish behaviour of their fellow comrades. No one should contemplate escape. I will teach all of you a lesson. As camp commandant I have a big responsibility. I am *samurai no kami* (warrior of the Gods). You are the enemy of our great nation. You are the enemies of Imperialist Ruler of Japan. When you took up arms against our great nation you gave up your right to live. You live now because we need labour. Otherwise will all be dead now. Understand. Obedience. You no obey. I make punishment.'

Colonel Sugihara stopped abruptly and pointed his sword at random to three of the assembled prisoners. Then barked out an order in Japanese. The guards jumped into action. They knew what to do. They had done it many times before.

Among the three prisoners dragged to the posts was Charlie. Each was hauled up and tied in such a manner that their toes barely touched the ground. As this was being done, the rest of the prisoners sent out a howl of protest. This made the camp commandant angrier. He barked out another order in rapid Japanese to one of the guards. The guard ran over to one of the posts, cut down a prisoner, and half dragged the man to where Colonel Sugihara was standing and made him bow down in a kneeling position. Colonel Sugihara took two steps forward and with one mighty heave brought the glinting blade down on the kneeling man and beheaded him.

'You see?' Colonel Sugihara pointed his sword at the crumpled remains of the man he had just slain whose blood was gushing at his feet. 'He was alive but now he is dead.'

Another angry protest went up from the prisoners. Colonel Sugihara stared at the assembled men and indicated with his sword to the same guard for the next prisoner to be cut down and brought to him. He then executed the second prisoner in the same way as the first. This time the prisoners were silent. The camp commandant strutted around brandishing his sword and raving and ranting again. A few minutes later his tirade stopped abruptly. The assembled men hoped it was the end of their camp commandant's bloodletting. They were wrong.

'He too was alive. Now he is dead. You dare to question the power and the might of the Imperialist Japanese Army? Understand. Obedience. Japanese superior. You die.' Again he pointed his sword to same guard for the third man to be brought to him. Charlie was dragged from his post and found himself kneeling at Colonel Sugihara's feet. At least his torture was at an end. His death would be swift. Charlie bent his head and waited for the blood stained sword to descend. His thoughts were with his loved ones in Ceylon.

But before the sword could descend, Captain Lee took three steps forward from the row he was standing in, came smartly to attention, and stood erect staring at Colonel Sugihara.

'I am a British Officer of His Majesty the King of England,' his voice rang out clear and strong.

'You, sir, are a sadistic and a barbaric animal who is a disgrace to any uniform you choose to wear. You bring shame and dishonour to your country and your Emperor.'

A guard moved forward to silence Captain Lee, hesitated, and fell back. Colonel Sugihara was totally surprised by this outburst. He lowered his sword slowly and turned his gaze on the British officer who had the impudence to insult him. Their eyes locked for a moment. Then he turned to the guard who had brought Charlie for execution.

'Take this man back,' he barked. Then pointed his sword at Captain Lee, 'Bring me that man.'

Charlie was taken unceremoniously back to the lined men and thrown to the ground. The guard then turned to the British officer who stood defiantly in isolation. Captain Lee did not wait for the guard to manhandle him but marched briskly forward and came to a halt a few paces from Colonel Sugihara.

'You dare to insult a Japanese officer? You are prepared to give up your life for a few brave words? Empty words?'

'I am prepared to die for my King and my country. I will die with courage, honour and dignity. You, sir, are a coward. You hide behind your uniform to cover the sadistic pleasure you get from torture and murder. When you die you will die like a coward. Whimpering and cringing and with dishonour. Your soul will not rest in peace and your dead ancestors will shun you. One day the world will know of the atrocities you have committed here and you will have to account not just to the free world but also to the Japanese nation.'

'More brave words. We shall see. I am son of samurai. Warrior of the Gods. *Samuria no kami.* When I die, I will die with honour. My spirit will live forever with my ancestors. I live by the sword, not by the bomb or the bullet. I will be a hero to the people of Japan.'

'You are a coward in the eyes of civilised people.'

'Take this man, strip him naked, and tie him to a post by his legs. We will now see how brave you are, you stupid British officer.'

Captain Lee was escorted to a post. He was beheaded while he hung upside down. The camp commandant stared at the assembled men. Then muttered the words to no one in particular.

'He died as a brave soldier should.' His blood lust satisfied, he turned on his heels and strode back into his hut.

Two hours after darkness had fallen, the storm broke. The prisoners had difficulty settling down. They were agitated and in a high state of excitement since the executions. The guards too were nervous and sensed there was more drama to come before the night was over.

The heavens opened with a savagery not witnessed in a long time as if the Gods wanted to cleanse all the blood that had soaked into the ground that day. Lightening snaked through the dark sky mixed with loud rumbles of thunder as torrents of water crashed down. Suddenly after one flash of lightening immediately followed a deafening explosion of thunder, the camp was pitched into total darkness. The generator had been knocked out. Simultaneously pandemonium broke out with the prisoners and guards rushing about. The moment Charlie had waited for had come. There was no time to waste if his plan was to work. To hesitate now would certainly mean failure and an ignominious POW camp death. Anything was preferable to that and he knew he would not get another opportunity.

Retrieving his bamboo dagger, Charlie raced to the machine gun tower farthest away from the guards' quarters. It took a few seconds longer, but the confusion gave him adequate cover to reach it before the panic stricken guards started to fire blindly in all directions. As he ducked and weaved through the mass of bodies, it felt like he was never going to get to the tower unnoticed by the sentry manning it. He fell to the ground and waited for the next rumble of thunder. The majority of the prisoners were charging towards the main gates and many were being hit by the bullets flying around.

When the next clap of thunder came, he climbed the platform as swiftly as he could and reached the top before the sentry spotted him. But when the sentry did see him it was too late. Charlie sank the bamboo dagger into the sentry's neck and eased him to the platform floor.

By now the whole camp was in total confusion with prisoners and guards screaming and shouting, and the staccato sound of the machine guns adding to the sporadic burst of rifle fire.

Charlie pointed the machine gun he had captured in the direction of the guards' quarters and kept firing until the clip jammed. He could not see if he had hit any of the guards in the darkness but it was time to get the hell out of there. He clambered out the other side, dropped ten feet into the rain-sodden ground, and ran to freedom. His plan had worked to perfection so far but Captain Lee was not there to smell the sweet smell of success.

Stumbling in the pitch blackness Charlie moved as swiftly as he could to put as much distance between himself and the camp as he ran blindly towards the dense undergrowth. There were bullets whizzing around him but he made his escape without a scratch. He knew he had to put as much distance as he could from the search parties that would come after him by first light. Charlie headed in the direction of the river as they had planned.

His commander had sacrificed his life in the hope that Charlie stood a better chance than him in getting back to allied lines. Perhaps it was Captain Lee's way of evening out the score for the number of times Charlie was instrumental in saving his own life and the lives of his comrades by using the jungle craft he had learned in the jungles of Ceylon. Perhaps Charlie was Captain Lee's last weapon. Perhaps he did what he did out of a strong sense of duty and loyalty to a fellow comrade. Now he was free and it was up to him to make the most of his freedom. He resolved to use all the cunning and instincts of a wild animal to escape from the enemy.

As soon as it was light, Charlie familiarised himself with his surroundings and immediately set about finding a suitable place to hide until the Japanese patrols gave up their search for escapees. He recognised the terrain he was in from their earlier skirmishes when sabotaging the supply trucks and their hit and run sorties. Before long he found what he thought would give him temporary protection from the elements and avoid being caught. A rocky outcrop.

He gouged out a hole big enough for his body with a stout branch and set about camouflaging the entrance with debris from the jungle. His lair was not unlike a cave and he reasoned no reptile would seek refuge in a freshly dug hole. They had come across many poisonous snakes during their campaign and marvelled that none of his comrades were bitten by one. When he finished his hideout he felt reasonably safe and soon his body gave way to much needed sleep.

Charlie awoke with a sudden jolt but he was in no danger. His subconscious mind was playing tricks with him. But while he slept, his feet had dislodged some of his hide and he realised that had there been any Japanese in the vicinity, they would have seen his feet sticking out. The Gods were still on his side. It was a good sign. He thought it best to get his bearings before darkness and moved cautiously in the direction of the river. He did not find his river. In his rush to freedom, Charlie realised he had lost his bearings and was hopelessly lost. He had not eaten anything since that ghastly meagre portion of half-cooked rice with the dead insects. Finding food was just as important for survival. His hunger would have to wait for another day as he was too close to that POW camp and it was too dangerous to wander about in the darkness.

He made another hideout for the next night and camouflaged himself better but it did not prevent him from getting a soaking from the heavy rain that fell during the night. Neither did he get much sleep. However, with the dawn came a brilliant blue sky and strong sunlight. The rain water he collected was enough to quench his thirst but he needed to find some food soon. The rain water was easy to come by in the hollows of broad-leaf plants, once he got rid of the snails and frogs that had sought shelter in them. He had heard that snails and frogs were a delicacy for the French but having never eaten them, he decided against it. Snails were never an item on their menu at home despite there being millions in their garden. His mother hated them. To her they were a pest that wreaked havoc amongst her plants. Besides he would need to build a fire and that was risky.

In his weakened condition, eating the many berries he saw would only cause him indigestion. He decided he would use the sun to navigate a route, and if possible, find some habitation. But then he found some plantains, mangoes and a few guavas that the fruit bats had missed.

Feeling better, Charlie was more optimistic but not having a weapon was a drawback. He made do with a stout stick to beat down the undergrowth and avoid the snakes he knew would be basking in the heat. The stick also steadied him from slipping and hurting himself. Any cuts and bruises could lead to infections but a twisted ankle or broken bones could spell disaster. The fury of the storm that hit the POW camp was evident everywhere by the number of fallen trees and the destruction left in its wake, but that too worked in Charlie's favour.

Towards the third day of freedom he found himself in dangerous terrain. Before him were deep gorges, fast flowing rivers, and tortuous trails made by animals that suddenly ended near a precipice. Sometimes he found himself in a maze that invariably led perilously to the edge of a steep gorge. There was no way forward. He had to back track and try all over again. To try and cross fast-flowing rivers in his condition would inevitably result in his death or being seriously battered against the rocks and injuring himself.

Progress had almost slowed to a stop but he had eluded his pursuers for the time being. Finding food was not a problem but there were always hidden dangers all around him. He made a fire, shielded from all sides by large boulders and cooked the fish he caught in rock pools.

Taking stock, it became clear to him that he had to turn back and find another place to cross this particular river. But he'd had a good hot meal, the first in months, and the prospect of a good night's sleep was something he looked forward to.

After many days battling through almost impenetrable jungle, Charlie found himself on the edge of a small village nestling on the bend of the river. After much deliberation, he decided to take a gamble and put his fate in the hands of the Gods again. He was exhausted; he needed rest; and he needed the assistance of the villagers if he was to reach the coast and the allies. But first he had to ascertain how far the coast was and what enemy activity was present in the area he was in.

While debating the matter, he was spotted by some villagers and soon surrounded by an excited crowd. Some stared at him in surprise while others conversed between themselves in Burmese.

'Me, English,' Charlie pointed to himself to see if anyone understood him. 'English soldier. Can you speak English?'

The crowd stopped jabbering. A moment later a man stepped forward.

'Me, English soldier. Bang, bang,' Charlie pointed his arms skyward pretending to fire a gun. 'Speak English?'

The man who stepped forward turned to his people and spoke rapidly in his native tongue. A youth from the throng stepped forward. He was dressed differently to the rest in a pair of shorts and white shirt.

'I speak English. I worked as a servant for an English family. Japanese soldiers came and took them away. I came back here. This is my village.'

'Please tell your people I am English and I need their help,' Charlie was relieved that someone understood him. 'I need food and rest for a few days. Also I will need assistance to reach the coast.'

The interpreter translated what Charlie had said. There followed a discussion between the interpreter and the Burmese spokesman in the crowd.

'You wait here. We must speak with the headman of the village. Harbouring an English soldier is big trouble for our people, you understand?'

'Yes, I understand,' said Charlie bowing his head in acknowledgement. He had gambled and now he had to wait to see if his gamble would pay off. He knew if the villages helped an escaped prisoner, the Japanese would subject them to terrible reprisals and many of their men, women and children would be killed as a result. At least there was no hostility towards him and amongst them was a boy who had worked for an English family. Charlie's hopes rose.

He got off the rock he was sitting on and lay down on the ground to await the verdict of the headman. He reasoned that if any Japanese were close to hand none of the villagers would have come near him. He felt strangely safe and with that feeling, the tension he was under in the past few days drained away and he fell into a deep sleep.

He did not know how long he had slept but when Charlie woke up, he found himself on a reed mat on the floor of a hut well away from the main cluster of rustic huts. Looking around him he guessed it was a storeroom of sorts by the various farming implements haphazardly stacked about the place.

'Ah, we thought you were dying.' Charlie looked in the direction of the voice to see the former houseboy watching him from the doorway. So it was no hallucination.

'Your headman, he will let me stay?' enquired Charlie with a smile. 'You will help me get to the coast?'

'The headman said we had no choice now. Once you entered our village it did not matter what we said to the Japanese soldiers, they would not believe us. They know we hate them and killing Burmese people comes easy to them. If they found you now, they will kill us all and burn down our houses. You looked bad and our headman said you would die soon. I was to wait until you were dead. Then we were to take you into the jungle and bury you.'

'I am sorry to disappoint you and your headman by not dying. I am very sorry I bring you big trouble.'

'Do not be sorry. I hate the Japanese. They rape our women. They kill our men. They eat our livestock. We do not have one pig or one fowl in our village. We have to hunt for meat in the jungle like stone age people. I like the English. They kill Japanese. We hope the English will liberate us. Make us free again.'

'Are there many Japanese here?'

'Yes, many. They come for our women. I want to kill them.'

'Let the English soldiers kill them.'

'Yes, English soldiers kill Japanese.'

'Will you help me?'

'Yes.'

'I need food and water.'

'I will bring it.' The former houseboy left the hut and returned with a bowl of rice and vegetables and a pitcher of water. Charlie ate the food and emptied the pitcher of water. The sleep and the food had made a new man of him.

'I need some clothes. Not like yours, like Burmese, and one of your straw hats but I have no money to pay you. If I look like Burmese I will have a better chance of not being caught.'

'I will bring it. I do not want money. You kill Japanese soldiers.'

'Thank you. How far is the sea?'

'Very far.'

'Will you take me?'

'No.'

'Why?'

'I have to look after my mother and my sisters. The soldiers killed my father and my brother. I was in the jungle when they came to my house. They would have killed me too.'

'I am sorry.'

'I have much sorrow too. That is why you must kill Japanese soldiers.'

'Can I stay for a while?'

'No, bad. You go tomorrow.'

'Okay, I leave tomorrow. Thank you for your kindness. Thank your headman too.'

'No thanks needed. You kill Japanese soldiers.'

The former houseboy disappeared into the darkness. Charlie lay down on the reed mat. He needed all the rest he could get before he started his trek to the coast.

The Burmese boy who had befriended Charlie came into the hut at the crack of dawn. He had brought with him the clothes of a peasant and a wide-brimmed conical hat made of reeds which the Burmese farmers wore in the fields. He also brought Charlie another generous portion of boiled rice and vegetables wrapped in plantain leaves and some fruit in a sack. He sat on his haunches and waited while Charlie finished his meal.

'I will take you past the Japanese camp about five or six miles from here. Then you go alone, English soldier. Be careful, many Japanese. There is another river,' he pointed vaguely to the jungle in a westward direction, 'much bigger. It goes to the sea.'

Charlie discarded some of his tattered clothes and wrapped the sarong around his waist and tied it firmly with a piece of string, then slipped on the tunic, and put on the conical hat. The boy nodded approval. He could easily pass as a peasant unless closely scrutinised. They left the village as soon as he was attired in his disguise.

The boy seemed to know every inch of the jungle around his village and the two of them made good speed until they got close to the Japanese camp. They had to go deeper into the dense vegetation to get past the many patrols. Soon it was time to bid his new benefactor farewell.

'Goodbye, English soldier. You kill many Japanese soldiers.'

'Goodbye, my friend. I have a lot to thank you for. The English will drive out your enemies. Your people will be free again. May the Gods watch over you, your mother and your sisters.'

Progress was much easier now but he still had to be alert to dodge enemy patrols. By studying the Burmese and their mannerisms he was able to pass himself off as one of the indigenous inhabitants of the region without drawing attention to himself. He learnt not to panic at the sight of a patrol he could not avoid, but bent down and walked like an elderly person.

Two days later he found himself at the lower reaches of the big river which was quite wide and with slower-moving water. He also saw little hamlets dotted on either side of its banks. From the number of flimsy boats on the water, he deduced this river was the main mode of transport in the area. If he could get a boat, he figured he could sail all the way to the coast. With so many fishermen on the river he could pass as another making a precarious living from the fish he caught. But the question was where could he get his boat? He had no money to buy one so he had to beg, borrow or steal one. He decided he would steal one as he felt he had made his contribution to the people of Burma. To do so he would have to watch and wait until the opportunity presented itself. If he got caught in the act, it would blow his cover so he had to plan his moves carefully.

A large tree by the river bank seemed the ideal place to observe the activity around him. Charlie pretended to be asleep. If any of the villagers spoke to him he pretended to be deaf and dumb and use sign language to say he was hungry. He had tested this ploy the day before and found it to be very effective on the monks at the Buddhist temple who took pity on him and gave him some food. But he realised he would need a sturdy boat. The flimsy craft he saw would break as soon as it hit the ocean swell.

Much later his patience was rewarded. The boat that suited his purposes came into view late that afternoon. He watched it being dragged on the river bank. It was sturdy, and long enough to conceal himself if greeted by other river travellers or a Japanese river patrol. He had made up his mind. Not too big, yet small enough not to be too conspicuous to the curious.

Time passed slowly but when nightfall came in a red crimson glow with thin fluffy clouds to help it over the horizon, Charlie waited patiently for the optimum moment to make his move. He watched the moon rise and cast its eerie shadows as the villagers settled down for the night. The conditions were perfect for the plans he had formulated in his mind. It was vital to put as much distance between himself and the boat owner before its loss was discovered. He regretted having to steal the boat but there was no other option open to him. These were poor people and he knew there would be a huge commotion when the owner discovered his boat had been stolen in the night. Charlie was riding his luck. He hoped it would hold for a little while longer.

Creeping stealthily, he edged closer to the boat but then a dog started to bark. Then another and another. It was a signal for all the dogs in the vicinity to give vent. Charlie was almost by the boat when he froze. A man came out of one of the huts and bellowed at the animals closest to his house, then picked up a rock and hurled it at the nearest dog. He found his target because the dog gave a yelp in pain. Charlie waited until the man went back into his house and quietly slid the boat into the water without too much difficulty. A moment later he was paddling silently to the middle of the river as he effortlessly sailed away.

Pacing his strokes like a marathon rower he let the flow of the water carry him down river. Progress was swift as the hours passed and by the first rays of the sun, Charlie had reached the delta of the river mouth, and the coast, he guessed, was not too far away. There were mangroves, small sand banks and small islands with tall grasses. He steered the boat away from the mangroves, looking for a suitable place to wait until darkness and headed towards a small island in the middle of the river, then realised that he would stick out like a sore thumb on a waiters hand to any passing traffic, so he changed direction and rowed towards the far bank.

As he got closer, he saw an oxbow to the side of the bank with dense vegetation overhanging the water. He manoeuvred his boat into the vegetation and camouflaged it as best he could. Tired as he was, yet exhilarated by the ease with which he had got as far as he had, he felt good. But a good rest was essential before he made his final dash to the sea.

Taking stock of his surroundings, he saw there were many outlets that meandered out to the sea but if he took the wrong one he could get lost and it could cost him many hours to find his way out.

The chill of the dawn was refreshing. Charlie bathed his sore hands in the cold water as he surveyed the scene around him. A few hundred yards inland he saw a huge tree with fruit bats squealing and squabbling as they staked their claims to their favourite branch on the tree. The tree itself was a mass of heaving activity. In the mangroves, cormorants had gathered to feed as they too vied for territory with the cranes and the herons and other river birds. Further on a pair of painted storks preened themselves as they warmed their bodies in the early morning sun, while further inland a few crows were cawing raucously, disturbing the idyllic scene. His attention was drawn to a brightly-coloured kingfisher by the gentle plop it made as it dived into the water not far from its safe haven.

There was no sign of human habitation or any other craft on the water. Charlie felt safe and relaxed. The sun warmed his aching and stiff limbs and soon he felt drowsy as the boat rocked gently. The horrors of war seemed a long way away. His luck had held on and he resolved to ride it while it lasted. He had to gamble again. Which route would take him to the sea the quickest? Would the fates still be kind to him? Eventually his weary body succumbed to sleep as he pondered his next course of action.

Some hours later Charlie awoke with a sudden start. He sat bolt upright, his body tense and nervous as he peered through the overhanging vegetation. The scene he saw was no different to the one he had witnessed that morning, except the painted storks had gone and so had the crows but the fruit bats were still squabbling with a few flying around. By the position of the sun he saw that it was past mid-afternoon.

Then he heard the noise that had woken him up so suddenly. The distant sound of a motor boat. At first it was barely audible but gradually the throbbing sound became louder as it came up the river from one of the outlets to the sea. It became obvious from the drone of its engines that a powerful craft was heading fast in his direction. There was nothing he could do but to stay where he was. He tried to get closer to the bank and deeper into the overhanging branches to get more cover, but was also mindful not to draw attention to his position by making big ripples.

Then he saw it. A Japanese gunboat was heading straight towards him. Charlie flattened himself at the bottom of his boat scarcely breathing waiting for the inevitable to happen. He braced himself as the gunboat became louder and his boat began to rock violently.

The seconds ticked by. Suddenly a machine gun opened fire with bullets crashing into the trees and bushes above him, smashing branches and scattering leaves as frightened birds took off into the air in all directions. Had they spotted him? The next burst of gunfire would be lower, and if so, it would undoubtedly riddle his boat with holes. The staccato of the machine gun continued as the Japanese gunboat was parallel to where he was concealed. Bullets thudded all around him.

Charlie heard a splash close to him and turned to see a huge crocodile slide into the water, then the scramble of other crocodiles racing to feed on the one just killed. Charlie had not seen any crocodiles that morning but now he saw many basking in the sunshine on the little islands in the river. Unwittingly, the Japanese saw the huge crocodile that was stalking Charlie and used it for target practise. He dropped back into the boat and held his breath.

As suddenly as the gunfire had started, it stopped. It was a very close call but by the sound of its engines, the gunboat was now going away from him. He waited a few moments before he took a quick peek when he thought it was safe to do so. The gunboat had rounded one of the islands in the middle of the river and was heading back the way it had come on the other side of the river.

As he took stock, he was amazed that none of the bullets had hit his boat. A miracle. Not only had the Japanese motor patrol saved him from becoming a crocodile meal, it had mapped out his route to the sea. He resolved to use the same route out of the delta taken by the gunboat but had to wait and make absolutely certain the coast was clear. While he did so he also kept a watchful eye on the other crocodiles in the vicinity.

About two hours before sunset, Charlie decided the time was right to leave his sanctuary. It was paramount he got to the sea before dark but the sluggish flow of the water meant he had to row more vigorously. Soon the smell of salt water in the air told him he was almost there. A little later he saw the white breakers glistening in the dying rays of the sun. The open sea was in front of Charlie and there was not a soul in sight. The omens looked good.

With a sudden surge of euphoria with adrenaline pumping through his veins, he paddled as hard as he could out to sea. He had made it against all the odds and there was no stopping him now. He would keep going until exhaustion overtook him.

Getting clear of the heavy breakers nearly capsized him a few times but Charlie eventually negotiated his way into the open sea. Heading in the direction of the setting sun he rowed steadily away from the Burmese coast. He welcomed the cool breezes that night as he lay exhausted in the middle of his boat but the unrelenting blistering heat from the sun made the next day's rowing slow.

He had no water to drink until the third day when he was woken from a fitful sleep by a sudden squall. Any water he had managed to collect at the bottom of his boat soon evaporated the next day.

If Charlie had been heading in the right direction, he knew now for certain that the sudden squall had blown him off course. He had hoped to reach one of the small islands in the Andaman Sea but he also guessed some of them could be occupied by the Japanese. But he had no options left. The friendly sea that had filled him with euphoria when he cleared the heavy breakers five days previously, was now his next enemy. He had no water and he had not eaten for nearly seven days. The little fluffy clouds he saw in the morning had been burned away by the heat of the day. The battle for survival was now much different to the one in the jungles of Burma.

He gave up rowing to conserve what energy he had and let the boat drift, but Charlie knew he was on the brink of death and soon began to lose consciousness. His mind started to hallucinate. Images of the horrors of the POW camp flashed through his mind. The cruel and barbaric face of Colonel Sugihara peered down at him as he lay at the bottom of the boat. Sometimes his sword was raised above his head, his manic eyes filled with hatred. At other times he saw Captain Lee hanging upside down and then his head rolling onto the bone dry ground in a pool of blood. Then the eyes took the shape of a big crocodile as it crept towards his inert body.

Blackness engulfed him intermittently. He could not tell if it was him or the darkness of the night. Once he thought he saw the lights of a ship in the distance but that too disappeared as quickly as he saw it. Did he imagine this or were these lights the stars in the sky? Charlie had lost his battle and sank into oblivion as his boat drifted aimlessly in a dark sea.

But again good fortune smiled on him. Charlie came round two days later and he slowly regained his bearings. Was this another hallucination? He was lying on crisp, white sheets on a bunk bed. He heard the sounds and the vibrations of the ship. Later he heard voices which sounded strange but the voices were not Japanese. Then he recognised one as a Texan drawl. He had seen many westerns in the cinemas in Ceylon. He realised he was saved from a watery grave. He lay there and relished in the sheer comfort he felt.

Later he was told he had been picked up by a US destroyer and the voice he heard speaking on the intercom belonged to the medic on board.

'Goddam it. I knew the limey would pull through. He is some tough cookie. Will be mighty interesting to hear what he has got to say.' The medic came off the intercom and turned his attention to Charlie.

'Ah, I see you are awake. You've been getting plenty of shut-eye for the past two days. Welcome aboard, buster. You are now in the safe hands of Uncle Sam. Almost got yourself blown up. You are one helluva lucky son of a gun. Relax, son, you don't have to worry none, no sir. We'll get you back into shape. My name is Jefferson and you are on board the US destroyer the *Detroit*. I am the medic on this rust bucket and we patrol this region from the Bay of Bengal to the Andaman Sea and the main shipping lines of the Indian Ocean. What's your name, boy?'

'Private Digby-Sloan, sir. Number 398729856.'

'What outfit are you from, Private?'

'Special Operations Expedition Forces in Burma, sir.'

'You were a long way off course out there in the middle of the goddam ocean. Not been fishing all on your lonesome

159

in that, that contraption you call a boat? It is mighty dangerous out there with all those Nips about. These islands are crawling with them,' Jefferson laughed at his own joke, his ruddy complexion getting ruddier as he laughed.

'As I said, we fished you out of the drink two days ago. We were looking for Nip mines and nearly blew you out of the water. What in Gawd's name were you doing out there, son?'

'I was after a great white, sir. Couldn't be bothered with the little fish.'

'Sense of humour too. I like that boy,' Jefferson scratched his head. 'A great white, huh? What in hell's name is a great white?'

'A shark, sir.'

'A goddam shark. Well, I'll be damned. You can tell me about that in the morning, fella. You just lie back and get your strength back, son.'

'Actually, sir, I escaped from a Jap POW camp and was trying to get back to allied lines. I need to get back to Allied Command as soon as possible. I have vital information to give to them.'

'Whoa there now, boy. You ain't in no fit condition to do anything right now. We will talk again in the morning. You've had a rough time. Whatever you have to say will keep till the morning. Perhaps you will make more sense. You have been rambling on since we fished you out. I cannot abide incoherence. Now, that's an order, Private. I'm in charge here. A great white shark, huh?' Jefferson muttered as he scratched his head again. 'The boy's had too much sun.'

Jefferson went out of the room, closing the door after him. Charlie gratefully sank back into his bunk and began to savour the clean, comfortable surroundings that had been denied him since they parachuted into Burma. It felt like light years since he had slept in a bed and was soon asleep again.

Chinks of sunlight poured into Charlie's cabin from a porthole when Jefferson O'Riley poked his head in. After a sumptuous breakfast, shave and a shower he was a new man again.

'Morning, soldier, feeling better?'

'Yes, sir.'

'Right, we shall have that talk now. One of our senior officers on board will be sitting with us.'

Jefferson O'Riley returned with another officer ten minutes later.

'I am Commander Sam Kelly. You've already been acquainted with Captain Jefferson O'Riley. I understand you have some vital intelligence for us, Private Digby-Sloan. Feeling up to it? Good, let's hear what you have to say, soldier. Start from the beginning and we'll take it from there.'

Commander Kelly was the opposite to his medic. He was a thickset man in his early fifties with a thinning head of close-cropped grey hair and a thick moustache. He pulled up a chair, as did his medic.

While Commander Kelly was cool and crisp in his manner, the good humour Charlie saw in Captain O'Riley's face the previous night was replaced by a serious look, but the warmth in his eyes was reassuring. Charlie told the officers about their mission in the jungles of Burma. How Captain Robert Lee and his commandos fought running battles with the enemy while blowing up communication lines, supply trucks and fuel dumps until their explosives and ammunition ran out; how his comrades were picked off, and finally being captured by the Japanese.

He told them about the POW camp run by Colonel Sugihara, and the torture, including the executions of Crawfie and Captain Lee. He told them about the large construction by the river, and its strategic value to the enemy who needed to bring supplies overland into that part of South Asia. The area was heavily fortified with bunkers, troops and heavy armaments on both sides of the river. Also aerial reconnaissance would be difficult due to the thick canopy of trees in rugged terrain. Any overland attack would result in heavy casualties with no guarantee of destroying the construction. Any aerial bombardment his commander, Captain Lee, thought, would be best carried out at dawn or during the night to prevent the loss of allied prisoners working on the construction.

Neither of the officers present spoke until Charlie had finished talking.

'This is one helluva story you got there, son. I reckon you deserve a medal,' Captain O'Riley was the first to speak.

'You can say that again,' agreed Commander Kelly. 'I'll get these details off to Allied Headquarters in India. Lord Louis Mountbatten is in charge of this theatre of conflict.'

'Instead of a medal, sir, I'd rather you saved one of these bombs for Colonel Sugihara's POW camp. That den of horror needs to be wiped off the face of this earth.'

After many coded messages between US and Allied Command Headquarters and British Intelligence, arrangements were made for Charlie to be sent to Delhi for further debriefing. Some weeks later, reports came to say that a strategic target in Burma had been destroyed. Charlie assumed it was the bridgehead he had reported on. From India, Charlie was sent back to England to convalesce. For the rest of the war he took no further action. He also picked up a Military Cross for his heroic contribution to the war in Burma.

CHAPTER FOURTEEN

While recuperating at a special army hospital in Buckinghamshire, Charlie formed a close friendship with an English nurse. Annette Miller was a gentle, caring woman who tried to help him get over his experiences in the jungles of Burma.

She was young and bright and her cheerful disposition went a long way in overcoming the traumas of war. Therapy helped, but on those leisurely daily walks in the grounds of the hospital, she would join him. Her personality did more to restore him back to normality than any of the counselling he got. Soon it became a regular routine and progressed gradually into something more than a duty.

Annette Miller began to spend more of her off-duty hours visiting Charlie, bringing him little gifts from the nearby village. Sometimes it was a book or some journal she thought might help Charlie to take his mind away from the flashbacks of the war. But she was not to know it was the memories of Penny Webster that had helped to keep him going during his worst moments when he would shut out reality and imagine he was in her arms. At such times he was a thousand miles away from the horrors around him.

Later, Annette would accompany him to the cinema, or invite him to her quarters for tea, or listen to the wireless. But Charlie was not aware that Annette had fallen in love with him and that her plans for the future invariably included him. She now had a future to build on. Something more permanent than the single life she led.

When Charlie moved into a flat, although Annette was officially still living in the nurses' quarters she moved in with him as it fitted in with her plans. She had it all worked out. A loving husband, a nice place to live in, and perhaps, a few children and her world would be complete. When her young body clung onto Charlie during those cold autumn nights she had visions of all those things happening to her. But to Charlie it was Penny he was making love to when he closed his eyes. If Annette sensed something, she thought it was the effects of the war that made Charlie act like he did. Like he was afraid of the future. His mind seemed far way when making love. Annette did not care as long as Charlie held her tight.

But one Saturday night they had returned from the pub and later when they made love he called her Penny at a crucial moment. Annette knew that her lovely Charlie had been making love to a woman called Penny and not her. This upset her. She realised that Charlie did not love her. At least not the way she loved him.

Their relationship was not the same again. Niggles began to precede minor irritations as the cracks in their relationship began to appear. Then began the mood swings with Charlie going to the pub on his own only to return to the flat to find Annette sulking. Charlie had not intended to let things get the way they had and in his mind he argued that this was not the way their lives ought to be. Annette countered that it was Charlie who was to blame. He did not deny it. He was aware he was being unchivalrous to a decent woman who had high expectations from him, and knowing he was not ready or able to make such commitments.

To continue in this way would only make matters worse. There was no long-term happiness for either of them. The time was fast approaching when they had to go their separate ways.

After one such visit to the pub, Annette went home to her parents the next morning. Charlie had made love to Penny Webster again. She left him a note saying it was best to separate for a while so that Charlie could sort out in his mind what he wanted out of their relationship. It was his choice. He could not have them both. She said she would wait patiently for him to contact her when he was ready.

Charlie wrote back to say he was unable to make any commitments, and it would be wrong for her to hold out much hope for the future with him. He appreciated all she had done for him and would hold a special place in his heart for her. She was a good woman and deserved more than he could offer her. He was deeply sorry for any disappointment he may have caused her but he could see no other way round. If he had caused her any hurt or pain it was unintentional and asked her to accept his sincere apologies.

Soon after being sent back to England from Burma, Charlie wrote to his mother to say he was okay. He said he had no plans to return home early. His war had been bad and he needed time to sort things out and when he was ready he would return. He sent them his love and hoped they were keeping well.

Unable to make the sort of commitment to Annette, however sweet and good natured and lovely as she was, he felt he had to make the break. She was too clinging and he felt claustrophobic. He could not find it in himself to nurture and cosset a beautiful English rose in his present state. He needed time to think.

Special Operations had plans for Charlie and his jungle skills but he had had his fill of the army. He had done his part and Ceylon was safe. He had completed his mission and the war games were over so far as he was concerned. He had done his duty and wanted nothing more to do with the kind of work they had in mind for him. He had experienced the senselessness and futility of war.

Looking at it dispassionately in the peace and quiet of the Lake District, everything looked different but in Burma it was kill or be killed, be it human or animal. The law of the jungle overruled all else. Survival was the name of the games played there. There were no referees to see if the rules were broken. Mistakes were paid for by death.

His thoughts of Annette Miller were clear. That chapter of his life was also closed. But he had one last important mission to complete before he returned to Ceylon.

On the day he returned to London, the mists had rolled in from the Thames. He booked into the Duke of Marlborough in Chelsea. He had promised Captain Lee that he would visit his wife if he did not survive the war. To express his sorrow and regret and to thank her for her love and understanding. To tell her he did his duty with honour and pride for King and country. She was to close this chapter in her life and get on with the next.

The train pulled out of Kings Cross station with much hissing and puffing of white smoke as it chugged its way into the countryside and the village of Tring in Hertfordshire. Charlie sat in his second class carriage and stared out of the window but he did not see the fields, or the cows, or the sheep, or the horses. He was thinking of Mrs Robert Lee. He should have visited her sooner.

Unconsciously, Charlie checked his jacket pocket to make sure he had not forgotten to pick up the little case he had placed on his bedside table the night before. The gesture was involuntary as he had done so several times before he left his room.

The train slowed down as it approached Tring station. He looked at his watch and noted that the journey had taken a little longer than he was advised it would take and made a mental note for his return. As he got out, he felt a cold, stiff breeze but the frost from the morning had melted.

He made a few enquiries and found the lane he was looking for. Then he saw the rustic wrought iron gate, proclaiming it to be Rose Cottage. He reached the front door through a winding pathway dotted with shrubs and a closely-pruned hedge. He hesitated as he observed the climbing roses framing the entrance with a few remaining rose hips from the summer. It was highly unlikely that this cottage was Captain Lee's choice, but that of his wife.

'Please Pull'. He did, and a bell rang somewhere inside. A few seconds later the door was opened by a pretty young woman with dark brown hair tied in a bun. Big brown eyes greeted him with a friendly, though quizzical smile. He guessed Mrs Lee to be in her late twenties.

'Yes?' she enquired politely.

'Mrs Lee? Good morning. Pardon me for intruding on your time. My name is Digby-Sloan. Charlie Digby-Sloan. Perhaps your husband mentioned my name in passing. Your husband was my commanding officer in Burma.'

Mrs Lee's smile brightened. 'No, my husband never mentioned your name. As a matter of fact my husband never spoke about any of the men he worked with. Maybe something to do with the army. Please do come in, Mr Digby-Sloan. My husband never spoke of the work he did in the army but I did know his last campaign was in Burma and it was classified top secret.' Mrs Lee led the way into the drawing room.

'Robert and I made a pact before we married. He was to leave army business behind him when he walked in the door. Anyone who knew Robert is welcome here. Please take a seat over there by the fire where you will find it more comfortable. This morning was pretty cold.'

Charlie looked around the room. It was well furnished and tastefully decorated. Comfortable, no cosy, was the word to describe that room. He could see that Mrs Lee was house proud. Everything was tidy and there was not a speck of dust to be seen. Taking pride of place on the mantelpiece was a gold-framed picture of Captain Robert Lee in full ceremonial dress. Next to it was another framed picture of himself and his wife, taken at their wedding. They made a handsome couple. There were other photographs of family members, small alabaster figurines and a little collection of curios. On the walls were several pictures of country scenes.

Charlie chose a chair next to fire and sat down.

'When I left London this morning it was still frosty.'

'I was about to enquire if you had had a long way to travel. I have not been to London since before Christmas. I found it rather depressing. They were still clearing up after the war.'

'We heard that London had taken a pounding. I have seen the mess the Germans have made,' replied Charlie feeling more at ease.

'Let me make us a pot of tea, we can talk then. I was about to have some when the doorbell rang. Please make yourself comfortable, I won't be a minute.'

A few minutes later Mrs Lee came in with a trolley. 'It was good of you to make the journey from London. Milk and sugar? Help yourself to a biscuit.'

'No milk, one sugar please.'

'Regretfully my husband and I did not spend much time together before he was killed in Burma,'

Mrs Lee spoke without any sign of emotion. 'Robert was a dedicated officer and very committed to his work. I knew that before I married him. Soon after we met war was declared, and as you might expect, that took even more of his time. I knew he was in Special Operations but nothing more. Very hush, hush. Just as well I wasn't curious, isn't it? Is your tea all right?'

'Perfect. High grown Ceylon tea.'

'Yes, Liptons. I get it from the Home and Colonial Stores right next to the train station. I prefer it to Darjeeling or the Chinese varieties. How did you guess it was Ceylon tea?'

'My father owns several tea plantations in Ceylon. I was born on one.'

'How extraordinary. But I must not digress. You are here about my husband. I had a letter from the War Office to say Robert was missing in action and was presumed dead. So cold and so heartless, and so clinical. I know that in times of war many men and women went missing. I've thought about how their loved ones managed to cope. There must be a softer way of breaking bad news to loved ones and families. When victory over Japan was announced, I expected Robert to come walking through that door. I thought he might have been taken prisoner.' Mrs Lee smiled but her eyes took on a peculiar brightness. 'You saw him die, didn't you?'

'Yes, Mrs Lee. I am sorry. Your husband was a very brave man, ma'am. Your husband died a hero. He saved my life. He gave up his life in a supreme act of bravery, and he gave up his life honourably as he carried out his duties.'

A long silence followed. Mrs Lee sat with her hands tightly clasped in her lap with her head bowed. She got a handkerchief from her skirt pocket dabbed her eyes and started talking again.

'I can now get on with the rest of my life. I now know for certain that Robert is not coming back. Like me, Robert's parents never gave up hope. I expect your loved ones were the same. He was their only child and they were very close. They were so proud of him when he passed out of Sandhurst. His Majesty the King was present at the ceremony. His parents have been so supportive to me, and so have my parents.'

'Do you have any brothers and sisters?'

'I had a brother. Michael was his name. When he was killed, he was only 22. Michael was reading philosophy at Cambridge when the war broke out. He joined the Royal Air Force without hesitation as did all his friends. He was really proud when he got his wings. Flew Spitfires. He prided himself on his skills. During the Battle of Britain he was based at Kenley in Surrey. They were hopelessly outnumbered but their spirits never broke. On his birthday the order came to scramble at about ten in the morning. They had been on a sortie the previous night but out they went. Michael's plane was shot to pieces and he ditched over the English Channel. So young with so much in front of him. Of the squadron that went up that morning, only one plane returned to base.'

'I am so sorry.'

'Michael was one of the "few" as Churchill described them. Those boys were brave too.'

Again there was a prolonged silence only to be broken by the trill of a robin that had perched on the window sill. A moment later another trill came in reply and it flew off to meet its mate.

'It's pretty around here.' Charlie felt the need to keep their conversation going.

'Yes, it is. The robins know that spring is almost here. They usually nest in my garden shed. If you like watching birds this is the place to be. The blackbirds usually nest in the yew tree by the shed. The wren in the box hedge at the front. Then there are the finches, song thrushes, magpies, jays, woodpeckers, and a variety of tits. It is so peaceful and quiet here I consider myself to very fortunate. This home has compensated me for the time Robert was away. I am pleased Robert did not die alone. He had a comrade with him when his end came.'

'I was fortunate to have him as my commanding officer. We depended on each other. We lived in each other's pockets. You get to know almost everything about your comrades. We formed a strong bond while we were in that jungle. When I was chosen at random for execution, Captain Lee took my place. He did not have to but he did. There was no hope in that POW camp. If you don't mind I'd rather not talk about it.'

'Robert was a kind and caring man, and a considerate and loving husband.'

'He had the respect of his men. He led from the front. He was a good soldier.'

'And you managed to escape.' It was a statement not a question.

'Yes.'

'Knowing my husband he probably had a good reason for putting himself in your place. He knew you had a better chance of getting out alive than he did. The regiment and his men came first. Duty and loyalty above all else. Robert put his regiment first and me second.' Mrs Lee got out of her chair and walked to the window. She stood looking out for a long time. Then she came back, sat down, crossed her legs, and looked at Charlie for something to say.

'You completed your mission?'

'I would like to think I did. My reason for coming to see you today was to give you this,' Charlie put his hand in his jacket pocket and pulled out the small case. 'I was given this but rightly it should have been given to Captain Lee. I want you to have it, ma'am.'

Mrs Lee took the case, opened it, and looked at the silver medal with its blue ribbon for a long time. 'The George Cross.'

Then with a sigh, she put it back in its case and closed the lid with a snap.

'This is an exceptionally kind and generous gesture, Mr Digby-Sloan.' The brightness he had seen earlier was back in her eyes as she returned the medal to Charlie.

'This medal was given to you and I cannot accept it. You would not have received such a high honour if you did not deserve it. Many brave men died in this war, and in my mind, I believe each one of them deserve our deep gratitude. You must keep it. Treasure it with pride. For yourself, and for your family, and for your friends, and for your comrades, and above all, for the country you fought for so valiantly. Wear it with dignity. If Robert was alive, it would have given him immense pleasure to know that one of his men won the Military Cross. I am extremely touched by your generous gesture.'

She bent forward and took Charlie's hands in hers and clasped them tightly. The moment was one of intense emotion for both of them.

'I expect you will be leaving for Ceylon soon?'

'Yes, I sail in two days' time.'

'It will be nice for you to get back to your family and friends. They will be very proud of what you did for your king and country, and especially returning as a highly decorated war hero. I assume you are married. Any children?'

'I am not married.'

'But perhaps you have a fiancé waiting for you?'

'I do have a special person in my life and that is the reason why I am eager to get back.' Charlie paused as he thought for a while. 'War changes people. I know I have. The country I left would have changed too. Getting back to the old routines is going to be a daunting task for me and I hope I won't be messing things up.' He was thinking of Penny. His thoughts were never far away from her. Could he resolve the impasse that made him leave the island that seems like many light years ago.

'People change all the time. Situations and circumstances never stand still but if your feelings for this lady are strong you are sure to weather whatever storms lay ahead. I am certain you will be fine even if it will take a little time to get back to the swing of things. I wish you all the happiness for the future' Bethany smiled reassuringly. Charlie did not wish to talk about Penny and was looking for a way to change the subject when Bethany broke the awkward silence.

'By the way, Robert spoke of a school friend by the name of Brett Carter. Apparently Brett gave up the opportunity of a brilliant career in the army to become a tea planter in Ceylon. Robert said Brett would have made a good Intelligence officer if he had gone with him to Sandhurst. He was an intelligent, sensitive, secretive and sometimes a very cunning individual and had the right qualities for that kind of work. But Brett had other ideas and it must have been a disappointment to his family when he did not. Robert thought it was a waste of good talent seeing that Brett came from a family with traditions of army careers. I was told that his grandfather was a Brigadier and his father was a Major but his father died relatively young of a heart attack on the eve of being promoted to Colonel. This may have had a bearing on his decision not to seek an army career. It was a sudden decision, his going to Ceylon. You probably know him.'

'Yes, I knew Brett Carter. My parents and the other planters tried to befriend him when he first arrived but he preferred to live outside our social circle. My sister Kylie played tennis with him occasionally but most of the young set did not have much to do with him, me included. I found him to be strange. Most thought he was weird. Brett Carter died in mysterious circumstances in September 1939. Soon after war was declared. We never knew the real reason.' Charlie was not going to tell Mrs Lee about the furore Brett's murder caused the planting community or the reasons as to why he was murdered or the hanging of the man who murdered him.

'Oh I'm sorry to hear this. His poor mother would have been devastated. Charlie, I hope you don't mind me calling you Charlie as you were close to my husband and I feel I have known you a long time. Charlie is a nice name. You may call me Bethany. It would have been nice to get to know you better...' her voice trailed off but her smile had all the warmth that only a woman could impart.

'It is such a pleasure and a privilege to have been able to meet the lady who played such an important role in the life of a man whom I will never forget. I owe my life to him.' Charlie stood up looking at his watch. 'Unfortunately time has flown by and if I'm to catch my train back to London I better leave now.'

'Well, I wouldn't want you to miss your train.'

'Good bye Bethany. You take good care of yourself.'

'Good bye Charlie. Thank you for coming. I trust you will have a safe journey home. Please drop me a line to let me know how you are getting on when you can spare the time.'

Charlie shook hands with Mrs Lee at the door and walked down the winding pathway. When he reached the rustic wrought iron gate he instinctively turned round and looked at the pretty cottage he had just left. Mrs Lee was at the door waiting to wave to him before he disappeared from sight. He guessed she followed the same routine each time Captain Lee left his charming wife.

Bethany Lee looked so alone and vulnerable in that white painted cottage.

CHAPTER FIFTEEN

'Ladies and Gentlemen.' His parents came into the drawing room where the assembled guests had gathered to welcome Charlie. The hum of conversation took a minute or two to subside. When his father had their attention, James started to speak again. 'Ladies and Gentlemen, Clara and I thank you for coming here tonight to welcome Charlie home. He put his life on the line for something he valued and he has come back to us safely. But a word of restraint please. War is not a pleasant subject for those who fought in it. I know Charlie would prefer not to talk about his experiences and I should be grateful if you would respect his wishes. That chapter of his life is closed. He acquitted himself with great courage and fortitude and came back to us as a hero. For his efforts he was decorated with the Military Cross. The highest honour, as far as I know, awarded to anyone on this island. Charlie now looks to the future. I ask you now to raise your glasses to drink a toast to his bravery and courage. To Charlie.'

'To Charlie,' went up the chorus. 'Hear, hear,' came cries from the rest while others clapped their hands. Then followed a lusty rendition of *For he's a jolly good fellow*.

James waited till the noise subsided. 'I have nothing more to say, ladies and gentlemen. Let the wine flow, let the music begin, and let the celebrations commence.'

The merry-making for Charlie's return was to go on till late into the night. Charlie endured the congratulations and the back-slapping for as long as he could. But with so many people about it was claustrophobic. He had to get out of there and escape to the far end of the verandah.

As he breathed in the cold, fresh air and the dampness of the mist that had formed in the valley below, it felt like old times again. However, the sights and sounds of the night, and the smell of the damp earth was also like being back in Burma again.

Suddenly he froze. His body went tense. A sixth-sense told him he was being watched. A tremor started at the base of his neck and went down his back. Was he being stalked by the enemy or some hungry wild animal? It did not matter. Both were cunning and blended into the surroundings only to reappear when it was too late. He had seen it happen. To survive, one had to be alert at all times. Failure meant death. But he realised it was a flashback to an incident in the war. He was not in the war zone but on the verandah of his home. He let out a deep breath of relief and felt the tension in his body ease.

Then he saw Penny framed in the doorway. She looked absolutely radiant, her red hair catching glints of light as the curls nestled around her neck and shoulders. He had eagerly looked for her but she was clustered by a small group at the far end of the room. She looked as beautiful as he had remembered her. A little older? No, it had nothing to do with age. There was something more subtle.

'Hello, Charlie.' Penny put her arms around him and kissed him gently on the cheek. 'Welcome home, soldier.' Then she hugged him tightly and buried her head in his shoulders.

They stood there while the world had stopped for them, content to hold each other again. Charlie felt the warmth of her body against him and was aware of her heaving breasts. The unique perfume of her body intoxicated him. No other woman had ever been able to replicate the sensual fragrance that drove his senses wild with desire. He felt the arousal rising in his loins and his pulse began to race. It was like old times and he wanted it to last forever. It was good to be back. But then she withdrew from his arms as she looked at him seriously.

'You've been avoiding me all evening. Why?' whispered Penny huskily.

'No, I have not.'

'Yes you have, Charlie. So much so it provoked a comment from Helen. Answer me truthfully.'

'You are a married woman, Penny. I could not trust myself to act normally after being away for so long. I have to be discreet, remember?'

'You do not have to be that discreet not to even acknowledge my existence. A simple hello would have been nice.'

'Do you think a simple hello would have been enough for us after all this time?' Charlie's voice was hoarse with emotion. He took a deep breath. 'There will never be simple hellos where we are concerned and you know it, my love. I've wanted you every day and every night while I've been away. I could have made a fool of myself with so many people about.'

'Very considerate of you.'

'Do you still feel the same about me as you did before?'

'I don't rightly know, Charlie. You see Philip has been exceptionally good to me, and my life has changed in more ways than you can imagine.'

'How come? You are still here. I am back. So what is the problem?'

'There are complications, Charlie. We have to talk but this not the time or the place.'

'Yes, let's meet somewhere private. We have much catching up to do. My feelings for you have not changed. You comforted me in my darkest hours.'

'You were not very far from my thoughts either, Charlie.'

But the magic of their embrace had gone. It was never like this before. Penny wanted an answer to one burning question. 'Did you meet many girls in England?'

'I was in the army and it was no vacation.'

'You did not answer my question, Charlie.'

'I had not joined a seminary. What kind of question is this? Of course I did,' Charlie spoke matter of factly.

'And did you love them like you loved me?'

'No.'

'Did you have sex with any of them?'

'Of course I did. It was merely a physical need. There was no emotional commitment.'

'Oh,' Penny recoiled as if she had been slapped in the face. 'At least you are honest, Charlie.'

'And what about you?'

'I was not unfaithful to you.'

'Listen, Penny. I did not think I was being unfaithful to you. I had a physical need to satisfy. In those fleeting moments it was only physical release. I am human and I am not perfect. It happened after I came back from Burma. The war may have had something to do with this but I make no excuses. There was death all around us. Everyone was living for the moment. Nothing was long term. I was a different person living under abnormal conditions. I was in a state of mind where I sought instant gratification. Whether it was eating good food, or drinking, or experiencing physical pleasure. Life was cheap. Life was short. Nothing made sense. Not unlike it was with you when Philip became ill.'

'And you hope there is a future for us, Charlie? That you can just turn up and continue from where you left off?'

'Yes, I still love you.'

'Like before? Somehow I don't think that will be possible. As I said there have been complications in my life too. There is something you need to know about me. I'd rather you heard it from me than from someone else. We need to talk soon. You have been honest with me and I will be honest with you. What I have to tell you is good so don't jump to any wrong conclusions. I must go now before everybody starts to wonder where I have got to. I would like us to meet tomorrow in Little England.'

'Where?'

'In the Grand. In the lobby at about tea time. Good night Charlie. I am glad you returned home safely.'

Penny turned on her heels and went back in.

Charlie had been waiting for some time when Penny walked into the Grand Hotel. He watched her come towards him with a smile on her face but she was not alone. With her was a little fair-haired boy of about four.

'Hello Charlie, I hope I haven't kept you waiting long. This little boy is Toby. Toby say hello to Charlie.'

'Hello, Charlie,' the boy looked at Charlie and smiled.

'Hello, Toby.'

'I think you will find some new comics in the rack at the far end, Toby. See if you can find any. I have to talk with Charlie.'

'Okay, Mummy.' Toby was off like a shot, found a few comics, sat on the floor and was happy.

'I said I had something to tell you, Charlie. Toby is your son.' Penny did not waste any time but told him about how she found she was pregnant soon after Charlie left for England; breaking the news to Philip; Philip's acceptance of Toby as his son; and how they had been getting on as a family. Nobody knew that Toby was Charlie's son.

'You and Toby and I can go back to England and live as a family. You do not have to stay with Philip now that I am here, Penny.'

'That is not possible. Philip has been so good to me. He has forgiven me for all my sins. I have a duty by that man. He is so good and generous, and treats Toby as his own. I have to think of Toby's future. He is safe and secure here. I've never had a home before and Kandalami is my home, and I have no intention of wrecking all our lives now. Not ours, nor your family. Think of what will happen if all this was to be made public. Think what this scandal will do to so many. Be rational, Charlie.'

'I don't want to be rational. I love you, Penny. I always have and always will.'

'Come off it, Charlie. You do not know what the word love means.'

'Oh, so that is it. You changed so quickly last night when I admitted to having sex with another woman. It meant nothing to me. When I made love to Annette it was you I was making love to.'

'Did you not think about how these women felt? How could you be so insensitive to those poor women? I'm sure they loved and you dumped them when it suited you. Charlie please don't set yourself up as paragon of virtue. As far as I am concerned you and I will never be the way we were. It cannot happen now. I was dealing with a situation as I thought best. Like you in the jungle. No, not like you in the jungle, but I was surviving too, to protect the life I created. This was my main responsibility. Remember, you were not around. You chose to go out there. I did not push you. You may have got killed out there.'

'But you still love me, don't you, Penny?'

'This may sound hard-hearted but I don't love you anymore.'

'Nonsense.'

'Don't protest too strongly, Charlie. You could not have loved me as much as you claim. You are a handsome and virile man and in the prime of your life, and there will be other pretty things who will lure you into their beds. I can't handle the rejection, the humiliation, or the torment. Always wondering who the next one will be. It is better this way.'

'I told you. I was not in love with these women.'

'Come on, Charlie, who are you kidding? How could you embrace these women, and do the things you did and still maintain they did not mean anything to you? I cannot believe you could be so callous as you sound. You do not know the meaning of love. Now it is your stubborn pride that spurs you on. You cannot accept the fact that there is no love in me for you and I am being honest with you. Now be honest with yourself. Find yourself a nice woman and get on with your life. We have both moved on, don't you see? We cannot get back to the way we were. I have got to go. Toby is getting restless. When I say I am glad you are back I sincerely mean it, but there is no more love in me for you. Sorry.'

Penny got up and went to Toby. 'Come on, Toby, let's go to Cargills and see if we can get ourselves a kite. Simeon will show you how to fly it when we get home. Wave goodbye to Charlie.'

Toby waved to Charlie and they were gone.

Charlie could not believe what had taken place. He refused to believe that Penny had gone out of his life. He needed her. He worshipped her. She was with him throughout the war. She was the one thing that kept him going. Charlie was absolutely devastated.

Penny had tears in her eyes which she wiped away with her hands. 'Why are you crying, Mummy?'

'I am not crying, Toby. A fly must have got in my eye.'

The sleek sports car darted in and out of sight as it climbed its way towards Diyalami. As it got closer, Charlie recognised his brother Rupert driving it. Charlie was seated on the verandah, his feet resting on the coffee table, having his second beer of the morning. Rupert parked his car by the main entrance and strode into the house.

'Hello, Rupert, nice motor you've got there. MG Roadster if I'm not mistaken?'

'Hello, Charlie. Spot on. A beautiful mover even on these estate roads. Simply glides around these sharp bends and handles the gradients effortlessly. I think Dad has ordered you one which you should have very soon. Oh, it was meant to be a surprise. Sorry.'

'That is good of Dad. All the young blades in England are driving these now. Very popular for impressing the ladies. What brings you over? No trouble I hope? You are just in time for a beer. That one,' he pointed to an unopened one on the coffee table, 'is still cold. Dad and Mum are out. Mentioned something about golf.'

'The Mile High is very popular these days. There's even talk of restricting its membership. Actually I came to see you. Jenny and I did not see you at the Webster's last Sunday. There were people waiting to meet you and I must say they were rather disappointed at not finding you there. You are a celebrity now, brother dear. I trust you can cope with all the hero worship?'

Charlie shrugged his shoulders and waved his brother into the seat next to him. 'If you mean the medal and all that stuff it means nothing to me. I was very surprised to get it. What I did I had to do. Nothing more, nothing less.'

'Don't go putting yourself down. They don't go giving medals like that willy-nilly. You must have done some pretty spectacular things to earn yourself a Military Cross. Enjoy the fame. You've earned it.'

'I'm in no mood for socialising. I'm quite happy as I am.'

'Never mind, eh. The Easter Ball will be here soon. I expect you will be there. You used to have great fun if my memory serves me right.'

'We will see. Were there many at Kandalami? Not like the Websters to have open house.'

Charlie had not intended enquiring about the Websters.

'Philip is a bit of a drag but no one can say that about Penny. She is so vivacious and spontaneous. They've changed so much since they had their son. Have you seen him?'

'Yes, I saw him with Penny at Little England. Nice little chap.'

'Looks the spitting image of you at that age, or so mother thinks. Fancy saying something like that. It's a good thing she restrains herself when Penny and Philip are about. If you weren't thousands of miles away,' Rupert laughed at the thought of his brother being the father of Penny's son, 'you would have had some serious explaining to do. You know what the gossips are like, especially as you were seen in her company prior to your departure. They named him Tobias. Sounds biblical. It was her father's name.'

'Really? Nice name. I like it. Want another beer?'

'Don't mind if I do.' Charlie went to the icebox and got two bottles.

'Tell me about England, Charlie. Is it stacked up the way Mum and Dad say? You probably didn't have the time to see much of the country.'

'A bit. Most of the big cities were badly bombed by the Germans. They are still clearing up the rubble.'

'What were the girls like? You must have met a few you fancied? We were half wondering if you would bring an English bride with you.'

'Beautiful. You don't call them English roses for nothing.'

'But you didn't find one to marry and settle down?'

'You need someone special when it comes to marriage. Marriage is a commitment for life. The woman who would bear you your children. I did not meet anyone like that in England.'

'Was Burma as bad as some of the stories coming out of there?'

'Burma was very bad but I'd rather not talk about it if you don't mind. This is the life to have. Sitting here without a care in the world sipping cold beer and watching the world go round.'

The brothers chatted on. Rupert declined to stay for lunch saying he had jobs to do. Charlie got drunk and fell asleep in his chair.

Seeking solace from a bottle was fine as long as Charlie stayed drunk but as soon as he sobered up the futility of what the future held for him seemed daunting and desolate.

Penny did not want him anymore. It had to be some dreadful mistake. They had a son now but instead of bringing them closer, it only served to drive a wedge between them. There was something very wrong that he could not comprehend.

The next time Penny and Charlie met, it was at the Easter Ball held at St Andrews Hotel in Little England. It was the highlight of the social calendar for all the colonial expatriates in that enclave in the mountains. As soon as the band struck up, Charlie lost no time in asking Penny for a dance. There was no way she could refuse as she was with Rupert, Jenny, Kylie and his parents.

'Can we talk while we dance?'

'Only if you behave yourself. Talk if you want to, Charlie, but we cannot turn the clock back. Why don't we settle for the happy memories we have. Our son is living proof of happier times so why go and spoil it all now? Pride goes before a fall. You've heard the expression before. We can avoid that but we cannot be lovers again. Can we not be friends for the sake of our son?'

'We cannot be friends. We can only be lovers. You have not been listening to me.'

'I have said all there is to say tonight. When this dance is over please don't follow me to our table. A blazing row now will only spoil things.'

Penny returned to her table. Charlie started to follow her but stopped and watched her. Then he turned abruptly and went to the bar.

'What was all that about?' enquired Jenny. 'You two looked so serious. If I didn't know you and Philip are so happily married I would say you had a lovers tiff.'

'What nonsense, Jenny,' Rupert admonished his wife gently and laughed as if to diffuse the curtness in his voice. 'If I had your imagination I'd be writing books instead of growing tea. I think it is my turn to dance with you, Penny. May I please?' Rupert escorted Penny towards the dance floor to a miffed expression on Jenny's face. Again Penny was in control and she was able to avert an embarrassing row in public.

'Hello, Charlie. I hope you don't think of me being forward by not following the correct etiquette I was taught at school by coming up to you like this. It would have been considered importunate if my school mistress saw me,' giggled a young blonde as she sat on the bar stool next to Charlie.

'Hello, gorgeous. Is your school mistress here with you tonight?'

'Not to the best of my knowledge,' said the still giggling blonde. 'But I don't give a damn if she is.'

'Neither do I,' said Charlie with a wink. 'Have we met before? You look vaguely familiar.'

'Of course you know me, Charlie, but I have grown up since we last saw each other. I am Fiona. Fiona Stirling.'

'Goodness me, so it is. You've certainly grown up, Fiona. From a chrysalis into a beautiful butterfly. Can I get you a drink? What is your brother Kerry up to these days?'

'Kerry is in Scotland. He joined the Dragoons and I shall be going to Scotland very soon. My parents think I should go to university as there is no scope for that here. I hope to be reading art and architecture there. I think I have had one too many already. I've been watching you all evening but I needed some Dutch courage to come over and talk to you. Our big war hero seems not to be enjoying the Easter Ball. In fact, you don't look very happy at all. I thought I ought to come over and cheer you up.'

The Easter Ball was one of the highlights of the social calendar for most of the colonial expatriates in the small enclave up in the mountains. It gave the women the opportunity to dress up in fine ball gowns and deck themselves in their most expensive jewels.

Charlie signalled to the bar steward, 'A drink for the lady, please. What will you have?'.

'I was drinking gin and Indian tonic.'

'A gin and tonic for the lady and a double whisky and soda for me. Steward, make that a double gin and Indian tonic.'

'I'm not sure I should have any more to drink. I get giggly and flirty if I drink too much.'

'I've ordered it now but you don't have to drink it if you don't want to. Why does a young lady like you want to spend time with me? You should be the toast of every red-blooded young man in town.'

'Don't be silly, Charlie. You are not old. Just a few years older than me. Mature but definitely not old. The crowd I'm with is so boring. They play silly games and act childish but you are a man of the world. A war hero. Brooding, and dare I say it, sexy. I like men who are brooding and sexy. All my friends look at you with awe. They all know you won the Military Cross in Burma. Do you find my presence boring?'

'Absolutely not. I must admit I was in the dumps so let's see if we can do something to cheer ourselves up.'

'Right. Where shall we start?' Fiona was flirting outrageously with Charlie. 'Perhaps a dance or two to the throbbing music will liven things up a bit. If that does not work I shall have to think of something else.'

'I put myself entirely in your hands, Fiona. Do whatever you wish.'

'I cannot do it all by myself. It needs two.'

'Okay, let's start with a dance and take it from there.'

To hell with Penny Webster. Jealousy had got the better of her. So what if he had made love to other women while he was out of the island. What did she expect? He had not joined a seminary. He was not impotent like her husband. Anyway it was Penny who had seduced him. Now she blames him for sleeping with other women. She wanted the best of both worlds and now the boot was on the other foot. He resolved that he was not going to get depressed from now on.

The signals sent out by Fiona could not be mistaken. She was out for a night of pleasure. As they danced, she clung to him. She hugged him tightly and pressed her breasts against him as she snuggled up to him. She was young and wholesome and normal. They had too much to drink and as they danced the night away they were oblivious to the knowing looks, nudges and suggestive remarks, or the sadness in Penny's eyes. Charlie and Fiona were having a great time while Penny sat through a wretched evening.

Towards dawn, Charlie and Fiona left the St Andrews Hotel from a side entrance and went up to his room at the Grand. They were not to emerge from there until tea time. In those few hours Charlie had managed to get Penny out of his mind.

But his resolution was not to last. Deciding that he could talk Penny round Charlie went to Little England. He resolved that he would stay there until Penny showed up. She liked to shop.

She turned up on the Saturday. But try as he might, Penny was not having anything more to do with him. To force matters to a head would only have caused a row in public which was to be avoided at all costs. And Toby was with her.

Clara and James too had noticed the change in their older son. Perhaps he had difficulty in settling down after the war. He had learned a hard lesson, that the world was a complex place to live in. But they guessed there was more to his sudden change. The moods of despair they saw when his guard was down was something new but their attempts to try and shake him out of his brooding was met with stony silence, or comments of indifference. Charlie was wrestling with something that went deeper than the war and they hoped it could be resolved soon. Until then all they could do was wait and watch from a distance. So unlike their Charlie.

CHAPTER SIXTEEN

'Come on Charlie, what is the matter with you these days? You drink too much. You are surly and your appearance does not do you much credit. You may not realise the effect you have on the rest of us. Excuse me for saying this but someone has to try and make you snap out of whatever is bothering you. You are not the only one who contributed to the war effort. We were spared when millions perished in this senseless war.' Kylie looked worried as she joined her brother on the verandah. She felt she had to do something before the rot set in too deep.

Charlie had turned into a drunk and it was not a pretty sight. Their parents said nothing but she saw how worried they were by the glances they threw in his direction. She decided to shake her brother out of the depression that had engulfed him.

'Sorry, Kylie. I apologise if I look a mess. Must try harder.'

'I think you ought to. You not only have a responsibility to yourself but to those around you. What's got into you lately? You weren't like this when you first arrived from Europe. What has made you like this? You look awful and it breaks our parents' hearts to see you like this. You are a man, a brave soldier, and a decorated war hero. If I have to pry into your mind I will do so if I think I can help you. We all love you dearly.'

'I guess I am drowning myself in self-pity. You are right when you think it has nothing to do with the war. I wish I could talk about it. I wish I had someone to turn to but there is no one who can help me.'

'You must help yourself, then. Why can't you tell me about it. I will listen. Sometimes talking can help. It has helped me.'

'Not that simple, Kylie. My problem is a big one.'

'Of course big problems are not easy to deal with, but to run away from one is not the way we Digby-Sloans go about things, be they big or small. Why don't you try me? I have all day and all night if need be.'

'Some day, but not today.'

'All right. Get out of that chair. Go for a run or a swim. I am going out.'

'I am going back to Glencoe. Perhaps it is best. I don't want to upset our parents.'

'Then I will see you at Glencoe. We have to try to sort this out. Between you and me. You know I will give my life for you if I can sort out whatever troubles you have.'

'Thank you, I do appreciate your concern for me.'

When Kylie got to Glencoe it was pretty late. She had gone to visit Rupert and his wife Jenny and had stayed for dinner.

Before Charlie went to his estate, he had taken his sister's advice. He went for a run but gave up quickly. He was unfit from too much alcohol. Instead he went for swim in the cold water of the lake. Then showered and shaved and made himself presentable. But when he got to Glencoe he started drinking again.

Kylie sat in a chair close to him. 'Right. I'm ready to have that chat with you but first, let me tell you about one of my big problems. It may help you to unburden whatever has made you so depressed these last few months. Well, while you were off the island, I met a lovely guy. He was an American GI. A doctor at the American Forces Hospital in Kandy. I worked as an auxiliary nurse there.'

Charlie looked at his sister. She was no longer a young girl but a mature woman. Self-assured, independent and forthright. He wondered what this beautiful woman knew of personal traumas. But he also saw the strength of character that he had seen as a child trying to fight her corner against two older brothers. But he also saw a softness; an empathy of a kindred spirit that comes from those who have experienced hurt and sadness.

'Like you my sense of desolation comes from the heart, and the mind, and the soul, Charlie. I see it in your eyes. I have been to that place too. Vincent Malacini was the most remarkable man I have ever met. He was not like the thousands of love hungry Americans out there looking for women to satisfy their needs and then move on. He was gentle and caring, and he was devastatingly handsome and passionate. I was told Italian men are passionate and you can take my word, he was passionate. He could have had the pick of any girl he wanted. Well, if he thought he could get me he would have a long wait ahead of him.'

Kylie paused to see if her brother was interested in what she had to say. Charlie smiled. She had not seen him smile much recently. His sister knew how to get round her brothers, and for that matter, the rest of the family, from an early age. Not another one of her stories, he thought, and then he saw that she was serious.

'Of course I played hard to get but Vincent knew how to charm me. Anyway to cut a long story short I got to know him better while helping to treat the injured, and I fell in love with him. Madly, deeply, passionately. Yank or no Yank I did not know what hit me. I could hear the bells ringing in each of the churches I passed. Vincent felt the same way as me. He even went down on his knees and asked me to marry him.'

'So what happened?'

'He asked Dad for my hand in marriage, too. He was the sort of man you would have liked. I took him to Diyalami, the first and last American that visited us there and he fitted in with all our friends. He was also a very good clarinet player. At times it was rather hilarious trying to get mother to play jazz, or swing, or the blues while he improvised on his clarinet. I know Mum and Dad were fond of him.'

'So why did you not marry the guy?'

'Problems. He came from a large close-knit Catholic family. He was one of eight brothers and sisters. They were restaurateurs. Vincent's parents emigrated to the States from Italy soon after World War One and they practiced the customs of the old country, and all lived in a place called Brooklyn in New York. Vincent wanted me to go and live there with him after we were married. I suppose I could have coped with their religion but I also knew I could not fit into their Italian customs. Nor could I live in a concrete skyscraper and feel safe in those congested, crime-riddled streets. So different to this place. From what he said it sounded awful but he said he could not live anywhere else. Despite trying to make him change his mind he would not budge. I knew that I could not marry him. To add to my problems, Vincent was expected to marry a Catholic Italian girl. I would have been a total outsider. His parents were very proud that their youngest son went to medical college. He was expected to follow in his father's and his brothers' and sisters' footsteps, but his mother wanted something different for him. We talked a lot but we both knew in our hearts our marriage would have come apart at the seams because of these stresses and strains. Can you imagine what that would have done to the children we had?' The expression on Kylie's face and her hand gestures said more than her words could.

'So the war ended. Vincent went back home and married a Catholic Italian American girl and lives happily with many Catholic Italian American children in his beloved Brooklyn.'

'You are so wrong, Charlie. He is not married much to the disappointment of his mother. He is waiting for me to change my mind. He still writes to me but not as often as he once did. He says I broke his heart. He certainly broke mine. My decision not marry him was not made lightly. It still depresses me. There is this deep void in me and I try to overcome the loneliness I feel. We all have to put on brave faces and not crumble into little pieces. Being in love is the most beautiful feeling in the world but under those conditions it would have suffocated and died. The sadness we both suffer now is preferable to the anguish we could generate later. I think it is better this way.'

'Still regretting it though.'

'There will always be regrets, Charlie, but it does not hurt as much now. In time the hurt will go away. You will cope as each day passes.' Kylie got out of her chair and walked to the end of the verandah to gaze into the valley below. She saw the sky was a myriad of twinkling stars.

'So what is this big problem that has got you into this state? Perhaps I can help you pick up the pieces?'

'It's late. Excuse me if I have a few more drinks, Kylie. I need to sleep. My head is killing me. Perhaps I will tell you everything tomorrow.'

'Okay, Charlie, I'm very tired too. Listen, remember what I said to you before. I will give my life for you. You are very precious to me.'

'You are to me too.'

'I'm off to bed. See you tomorrow. Night, night.'

Kylie went off to bed. Charlie continued to drink.

Kylie had finished her toiletries, then admired her naked body in the full-length mirror. She liked what she saw. She had a good figure and she resolved to keep it that way. She got into bed and thought about her reminiscences of Vincent till she became drowsy and fell asleep.

Sometime later that night, she might have slept for an hour, or it could have been longer. Someone had come into her room, pulled off the covers and got into bed next her. She felt his hot naked body against her. She then realised it was her brother.

192

'Charlie? What the hell are you doing in my bed?'

'Penny, sweet Penny. My hot, sexy Penny. I knew you couldn't stay away from me. I knew you would come to me if I was patient. Oh, Penny you will never know what this means to me. I knew you could not resist me. Not after all those precious moments we had together. Ah, let me cuddle you. I'm no longer a drowning man and we can both live again. Please don't push me away.'

'I am not your Penny. Have you lost your mind? Charlie get a grip on yourself. You are raving like some demented lunatic.'

'Please don't reject me. Just this one last time. I beg you. Hold me, hold me the way you did before, Penny. You are the only woman who knows how to make love to a man such as me. You know how much I love you.' Charlie whispered incoherently.

'I am not Penny. What are you mumbling about?'

Charlie's whispering was incoherent. 'Please, I need you. Love me the way you always did. So gentle, so kind, so beautiful, so passionate. Please don't reject me. Just this once and I will die for you. I will go away and never bother you again. Please, Penny,' Charlie voice was hoarse with a desire he could not control. 'I want you. I want you now.'

Kylie was fully awake now. It was not some ghastly dream. Her brother seemed to have had a complete nervous breakdown. She did not know what to do. Her brother was suffering and she felt she had to do something to try and get him to realise that she was not Penny. But all to no avail. She put her arms around her brother and held him as tightly as she could.

'Calm down, Charlie.'

'Oh, Penny, oh, Penny, You came to me. I knew you would. Now I'm safe. Thank you my love. I want to love you like we did before. I want to kiss your nose, nibble your ears. I want to kiss your toes. I want to kiss your eyes; I want to kiss your thighs. I want to caress your breasts and feel the roundness of your bottom, you goddess of love. Oh God, it has been so long.'

'Do it Charlie, do it. I will take those demons out of your head. I will hold you tight. You are safe with me. Do it. Do whatever you want to do. I said I would give my life for you if I could. I will now keep that promise. My poor, poor Charlie.'

Charlie had had a complete nervous breakdown.

Much later.

'Charlie, Charlie, Charlie you poor boy what have they done to your mind? You are safe with me. Hush, you are safe. Your Penny is with you.' Kylie held her brother in her arms and rocked him to sleep. She had at last discovered what had driven him over the edge. 'You are no longer in the jungles of Burma. You're safe with me. Go to sleep. You are with Penny now.'

Nothing mattered any more. Kylie comforted her brother until sheer exhaustion overtook her and she too fell asleep with Charlie in her arms.

When she awoke in the half light of a chilly misty morning, she was alone in her bed. Was it all a dream? Was it just a nightmare? Had she imagined it? Then it gradually dawned on her that it was no dream. Everything that had taken place came into sharp focus. Charlie had fought to save their lives but he had paid a very heavy price in doing so. Kylie said she would give her life for him. She did not have to. Instead she gave him her body. In the cold light of day it did not matter. Nothing mattered if she was able to get those demons out of her brother's tortured mind. She realised that both their lives had imploded in a way that was hard to contemplate as a result of the price he paid in the jungles of Burma and being rejected by the only woman he really loved which had turned into a deadly obsession.

Much later and with great trepidation, Kylie went looking for her brother but Charlie was nowhere in the house. In a daze she checked all the rooms. Her brother had disappeared. Had he come to his senses and realised something very wrong had happened in the night. She went outside to see if his jeep was still there but that was missing from the spot he had parked it the night before.

Charlie had disappeared. It had rained in the night and the tyre tracks showed evidence that he had driven way at speed.

As the morning wore on Kylie wondered whether she should go looking for him but he could have gone anywhere. The Knuckles range of mountains was covered with a shroud of mist. Being surrounded by those mountains always made her feel safe and secure but this morning it was gloomy and sombre and forbidding.

Later that morning they found Charlie. He had hit a rock fall at Dragons Head Pass on the way to wherever he was running. He and his jeep were found in the ravine 400 feet below the narrow pass and he was dead.

Mercifully Charlie's war had finally ended.

THE END